TEASED TO DEATH

a Misty Newman mystery

Gina LaManna

TEASED TO DEATH

CHAPTER ONE

———

I punched the power button on the stereo. Barely visible through the feather boas and sequined gloves draped over the machine, the light blinked red as I selected the perfect song. A flutter of excitement rose in my stomach. An upbeat, spicy tune pulsed through the speakers.

"What is burlesque?" I punctuated the question with a sly smile through stained red lips. Glancing at the mirror-paneled walls, I took in my very own, sparkling new dance studio—the floors shiny, polished, and begging for eager feet.

However, as I spun around to answer my own question, a sinking feeling took over the pit of my stomach. The words died on my lips, and my excitement evaporated as quickly as it'd bubbled up. There was one very major thing missing.

Students.

I sighed. How depressing. I'd had the studio for a month, and this afternoon was supposed to be my first class. But amid numerous phone calls, ads in the newspaper, and posters slated around town, my class list contained nothing but a big, fat goose egg.

Trying to cheer myself up, I'd decided to run a practice class even though the room was empty. It wouldn't hurt to get some of the kinks out if I ever got a pupil to sign up for my Intro to Burlesque class. Plus, it always felt good to dance.

When, I reminded myself, *when* my first student signed up. It wasn't my fault that Little Lake was a closed-minded small town happy to bask in its humid summers and cozy, snowy winters, tucked safely into rural Minnesota—a town where Sunday Mass was a social event and gossip was the *most* important currency of the locals.

They just needed some time to warm up to the idea. But in all honesty, I wasn't sure that the class would ever be a success.

I extended one leg and touched my toes, letting the fire stretch through my calves and into my hamstrings. The burn was welcome.

God, I am so out of shape. It's been so long since...the incident.

"Burlesque is classy. It is the art of tease." I shook my hips tentatively to the beat. It'd been a while since I'd moved like this, a nice shake of the bum, hands snaking through my hair before letting it fall seductively around my shoulders.

The beat of the music picked up. I stepped in time around a chair, running my hand over the seat, swiveling my legs until I was seated *just so* on the edge. Lifting a satin-gloved hand, I slowly pulled on the fingertips, loosening the fit. Next came a shimmy, a shake, and in one smooth motion, I stood, flipped my hair back, and pulled off the glove with my teeth.

I swung the glove like a lasso above my head. As the song neared its climax, I peeled the other glove from my hand French style, spun in a circle, and tossed it behind me.

Bending over, butt in the air in nothing but spandex, I caught a glimpse of movement behind me.

What the... My heart raced.

I snapped into a standing position and turned around. Whoever was behind me had a perfect view of my bum. And it wasn't that I was shy about my body—I wasn't allowed to be, given my previous job consisted of dancing almost naked in front of strangers—but I also didn't make it a habit to greet strangers rear end first.

As I turned around, however, I realized it wasn't the first time we'd met. In fact, the man standing before me was *anything* but a stranger.

Leaning with a cocky confidence in the doorway, trim and muscular, Jax Adams' arms flexed as he began a slow clap. His hair stood up in chaotic intervals, but somehow he wore the chaos with boyish charm.

I narrowed my eyes, and his face burst into a grin.

"Misty Newman." His voice rolled like a pleasant, soothing thundercloud at midnight.

"Mr. Adams," I replied. "To what do I owe this honor?"

"It's been a while since I've seen you dance." His words were confident. He could probably get away with it only because his smile was so dang disarming. "It's nice."

He swung my satin glove in lazy circles. He must've caught it when I tossed it backward.

The man was trouble. *I knew* that for a fact, but still I had a hard time remembering the words I wanted to say. "Yeah, don't get any ideas, buster. And gimme that."

I held my hand out for the glove, which Jax tossed to me with a long stride forward.

"Oh, I've got plenty of ideas."

I blushed. "What are you doing here? If you want to sign up for my class, fine. If not, please leave my studio. The floors are clean, and I don't want you mucking things up."

Jax raised an eyebrow. "This time I'm not the one mucking things up."

I crossed my arms.

Jax took a step forward and put one hand on my arm. "I've mucked up plenty in my day, but this one's on you, honey."

I looked up into his crystal eyes, pure as an Icelandic glacier with the capacity to be just as frigid. His words jumbled in my head, and suddenly putting a sentence together became like something of a Rubik's Cube for my brain. Something about his familiar scent—the minty freshness of his aftershave—twisted my gut and brought back years of emotions. Despite the surge of frustration and hurt, there was still a bit of attraction that I hated to admit was alive and well.

"What do you mean?" I cleared my throat.

Jax, my high school boyfriend and first love, stepped close to me, his chest inches from mine. My heart leapt even though I wanted to cage it back and lock it away. My head was telling every part of my body *no, no, no!* But my body was more than ready to ignore the warning from my brain, judging by the warmth snaking through my veins.

"Jax, I…" I paused, my chest rising and falling with years of pent-up emotions. "Why are you here?"

He rested one hand in his pocket, shifting uneasily. Whiffs of lemon, crisp fall leaves, and freshly brewed coffee swirled in heavenly drifts around us. We were close enough that I could feel his hot breath steam down my neck. Goose bumps erupted over my legs. Even without touching, I felt years of anger disappear in a second, and all I wanted was for Jax to pull me into a hug.

"Jax, I—listen." I took a long sigh and prepared an apology. An explanation. But as I began to speak, he pulled away, and I saw confusion in his eyes.

He scratched his chin, looking uncomfortable. "Yes?"

"I'm glad you're here," I said. "And I really appreciate you stopping by. I've been busy since I arrived back in Little Lake, and I haven't had much time to catch up with people, what with getting the studio up and running..."

"Misty—"

"No, let me," I interrupted. "I know we have a bumpy and, uh, unresolved past—but I'd like for us to be friends." I finished my sentence in a rush, looking down at my toes. I suddenly felt very vulnerable, and I wondered if I should have been so forward.

Jax cleared his throat.

"Now would be a good time to say something," I urged, still stubbing my toe against the floor.

"Well, I appreciate the sentiment," Jax said, "but..."

"It's okay if you don't want to be friends. I'd understand completely." I shook my head. "I shouldn't have said anything. I just wanted you to know I'm sorry."

"This makes things very awkward," Jax said.

Now we were both looking away from each other, which was very difficult due to all the mirrors in the place. I caught a glance of my reflection—medium brown hair, long legs clad in fishnet stockings, and hazel eyes, now staring back at me with fear. The tension was so thick I could've sliced it with a butter knife.

"Let's just forget this ever happened. Truce?" I stuck out a hand and forced my eyes to meet his stare.

"I'm afraid it's not that easy," he said, pulling the hand from his pocket and crossing his arms over his chest. "Misty, I need to ask you some questions."

"About what?"

"I'm sorry about this," he said, his voice not one hundred percent convincing. He'd morphed from an awkward conversationalist to a calm and professional cop, which was cemented by the uniform he wore. After a long moment, he sighed and dropped my hand. "I need to ask you some questions about a murder."

My spine went rigid, and I was already kicking myself for thinking I ever wanted a hug from this man.

"Will you come down to the station so I can ask you a few questions?" he asked.

"What does a murder have to do with me?" I asked, hearing the tremble in my voice. "Why would you need to ask me questions?"

"The body was found in the alley behind your studio, strangled with a pair of fishnet stockings." Jax paused before locking eyes with me. "It'll be a few days before we get the DNA tests back, but if it turns out the tights are yours…"

Jax didn't need to complete the sentence for me to know exactly what would happen if the stockings were mine. I stumbled backward. "Jax, I didn't do anything. I don't even know what you're talking about. Whose murder?"

Jax reached forward and caught me just before I ended up in a heap on the floor. His muscular, familiar arms pulled me into a standing position.

"It's impossible," I murmured, still stuck on the notion that I could be arrested for a crime I didn't even know had been committed. "I have no idea what you're talking about."

"Misty, please cooperate," he said. "If you come down to the police station, we're just going to ask you a few questions about the murder of Anthony Jenkins. If you didn't do anything, then you have no need to worry—"

"No! Please, Jax, you have to believe me." My knees gave out, and I felt myself sinking to the floor again as I registered the victim's name. "I have no idea what you're talking about."

Jax's professional, clinical manner was unnerving. He'd changed from a reckless, wild boy into a law-upholding policeman. His eyes softened a bit as he reached forward and helped me to my feet. "Everything will be smoother if you cooperate."

"But Anthony was just my landlord. I've barely spoken to him at all since I came back to town. I don't understand why—how—I'm being taken in for questioning," I said, my hands trembling.

Jax ran a hand through his hair and exhaled loudly. "Please come with me. It won't take long."

"Can I at least put pants on?" I asked. I glanced down at my fishnet stockings, tiny leotard, and bare feet. The black feather boa, complete with sparkles, swung haphazardly from my neck.

He gestured for me to go ahead.

I wriggled quickly into a pair of sweats, my fingers shaking as I tied the waistband.

"Shall we?" he asked once I finished.

"I don't think I have a choice," I said, trying to put on a brave face on the outside. Because on the inside, I was full of fear.

He marched next to me in a long, uneasy silence down the hallway of my studio. I glanced toward the small office I'd worked so hard to make cozy, despite its less-than-ideal location at the far end of the hallway. The space was the size of a shoebox and would have better functioned as a broom closet, but I'd had to make do for the price. Plus, I didn't spend a lot of time in there. In fact, once I'd set it up two weeks ago, I hadn't gone back.

As we emerged into the sunlight outside, I did my best to ignore stares from shoppers as Jax led me past the parking lot the studio shared with the other stores in the small town center. Jax tried once or twice to make conversation, but I didn't take the bait.

"I'm sorry," he apologized.

"It's fine," I said shortly. I wasn't exactly sure how to feel at the moment, my words coming out clipped. I supposed there was a little bit of confusion, a little bit of anger, a little bit of terror—at the end of the day, this was all a giant misunderstanding. I just hoped the cops would see it that way too.

He turned to me as we reached his cruiser. "On the plus side, you look very nice," he said, breaking the tense silence once more. "I like what you've done to your hair."

I didn't respond, thinking instead that my hair might look nice for a mug shot at the rate things were going today.

Jax opened the door to the cop car.

I held my stance and looked him in the eye. "I'm going to talk to your sister about this."

"She'll hear about it one way or another," Jax said with a sigh. "Careful now, duck your head." Jax gently but firmly shoved me into the backseat.

Sitting in the back of the cop car, I felt as if I'd taken a soccer ball straight to the gut. Half of me wanted to puke. The other half wanted to cry until I was all sobbed out. There was also the frustrated half of me that wanted to call Jax some not-very-nice names.

But there was also a small part of me asking scary questions. *What's this all about?* Sure, I hadn't seen Jax in ten years, but it was obvious by the hard line of his jaw and the firm contours of his face that this was serious business.

"Do you think I did it?" I asked, my voice soft.

Jax surveyed me in the mirror, but his look wasn't one that might be exchanged between a man and a woman who'd once been intimate. Instead, his eyes scanned me like a cop, analyzing my actions, features, movements. The sterility of his gaze hurt the most, a realization that shocked me.

"I don't know, Misty," Jax said, shaking his head. "But it's my job to find out."

CHAPTER TWO

———

"Ms. Newman, may I ask you a question about your personal life before we start?"

"What sort of question?" I asked hesitantly.

Alfred Shnocklepops, an unfortunate name tagged to an unfortunate body, sat before me. The plump cop had a row of pimples across his forehead that vaguely resembled the Rockies, and his hairline had been receding since sixth grade.

"How many lovers have you taken since me?" His round eyes stared at me with alarming clarity.

I started. "What?"

"Relationships, Ms. Newman. How many relationships have you had since ours?" he asked with a sweeping gesture.

I glanced around the room where I'd been taken to answer a few questions. I'd been provided with coffee and water, and it seemed like the cops were trying their best to make me comfortable. Except for Alfie's probing questions, that is. "Alfie, we never *had* a relationship."

I was ashamed to admit that Alfred Shnocklepops had been my first kiss—not because of his looks but because of the reason behind the smooch. Looking back, it would've been nice if my first kiss would be a romantic moment, something sweet and memorable, with someone I loved.

Instead, Alfie and I had been two six-year-olds playing dodgeball on an old, rickety playground during recess. At the time, I had whipped the ball as hard as my scrawny arms could at none other than Jax—the elementary school heartthrob—but Alfred's big noggin got right smack dab in the way. It wasn't my fault his head was the size of a watermelon.

Little Alfred had proceeded to cry and scream and generally make a fuss for the rest of recess. Since I desperately didn't want him to tattle on me in front of Jax, I pleaded with him to reconsider his formal complaint to our teacher.

I've never been proud of it, but eventually Alfie agreed to a deal. His one condition, however, was that I give him a kiss. Which was the story of my first smooch.

"I see," Alfred said, after a mini stare-down. He tapped his pencil, *tsking* sadly, as if I were in denial of a special relationship we'd once had.

I made a sound in my throat, but I was trying to follow that old rule: if you can't say anything nice, don't say anything at all. A grunt didn't really count as *saying* anything.

"Let's move on." Alfred looked at his paper. "Where were you on the night of Anthony Jenkins's murder?"

I paused a moment to collect my thoughts. "You're going to have to be more specific. I have no idea *when* you're talking about. Today? Yesterday? Two weeks ago?"

"Last night. Anthony Jenkins's body was found in the alleyway outside of your studio this morning, and he was believed to have been killed late last night. Where were you?"

"I was at home." I crossed my arms. "Reading."

Alfred gazed me over. "Reading what?"

"Books." I sealed my lips shut.

"Can anyone vouch for you?" he asked.

"Yeah, a bottle of wine and a bowl of Froot Loops," I said.

"Now's not the time to be funny, Ms. Newman." Alfred's ears tinged a bit red. "Please tell me about your relationship with Anthony Jenkins."

"Anthony?" I still didn't see the connection. I didn't have a ton of feelings one way or another toward the guy. "He was my landlord. I barely knew him."

"That's not what we've heard," Alfie said with a hesitation.

"I don't know where you're getting your information. It's terrible that he was murdered, of course, but it wasn't like I was friends with the guy. We were business acquaintances." I was lying only a little bit to Alfie.

I'd interacted with Anthony once or twice outside of our business transactions, but only because he'd asked me out on a few dates. I'd always declined—he was *married!*—but I didn't want the guy *dead*. In fact, we'd struck a pretty sweet deal on my studio only a month before when I'd moved back to town from shiny Los Angeles. It was one of the reasons I'd made my way back to the Midwest in the first place. He'd given me a price on real estate that I couldn't refuse.

"So you're denying any relationship with the man?" Alfred looked a bit miffed, as if my *relationship* with the landlord was any of his business. Even though I wouldn't dream of even holding hands with Anthony Jenkins.

"I'm confused at this *relationship* you speak of," I said. "I moved back from LA a few weeks ago. I needed space for a studio, and he was the landlord of the Crossroads strip mall. It's in town, a prime location for a dance studio between Sweets Candy Store and the Beauteous Babe salon. We negotiated a good deal. Bam. Done. That's it. I paid him first and last month's rent early. I didn't owe him a dime."

Which was good, because I didn't have a dime. I'd funneled all my savings into ripping down the dusty old market previously occupying the space and turning it into a bright and sparkling dance studio. If I didn't succeed at teaching burlesque classes, I was in deep doo-doo. Right now I was able to afford Froot Loops and oatmeal, a relatively well-balanced meal in my book. It would be gourmet compared to the cardboard boxes I'd be eating if my classes didn't take off.

"What would you say if I knew that there was more between the two of you?" Alfred stared eerily into my eyes, as if waiting for the dirty truth to come out. A dirty truth that didn't exist.

"I don't know what you're talking about," I said, my body suddenly feeling weary. "Can I go? I have classes to teach."

Alfred's gaze didn't waver. "I'll need a list of the students in your class."

"Why?" The main reason I was hesitant to hand over that info was because of the fact that current enrollment numbers were a little on the low end—a.k.a Zero.

"Because the body was found just outside your studio, in the alley. Strangled with a pair of fishnet stockings. We'll know for sure in a few days if they're yours or not, but I do know that you're the only burlesque dancer in this entire town at the moment."

"Other people might have stockings," I said.

"We'll wait to see what the tests show," Alfie said, neither confirming nor denying my point. "I'll need a list of everyone who was inside your studio between last night and now. And, Ms. Newman, someone saw something, I guarantee it. We'll get to the bottom of this."

"Good." I raised my chin. "I hope you discover the killer, because it wasn't me. For the record, I have no students currently, and nobody was in the building until Jax asked me to come in for questioning."

He sniffed, as if my acknowledging Jax was a low blow to his ego. Alfie's gaze was cold and stern, as if he believed my reappearance in town had caused someone's death. The thought churned my stomach, and I regretted the second bowl of Froot Loops I'd consumed for breakfast.

"Do you have a reason to keep me here any longer?" I forced myself to keep my gaze strong.

Grudgingly, Alfred stood up. "Don't leave town, Ms. Newman."

"I won't. I didn't do anything wrong," I said, meeting his gaze. Though in my heart I knew I was innocent, Alfred's unconvinced look twisted my stomach in knots as he led me from the room.

CHAPTER THREE

———

I couldn't bring myself to go past the studio on my way home. Not only could I not bear the thought of seeing crime scene crews tear the place apart—not after my heart and soul and money had been poured into the place just as firmly as the cement in the floors—but I also physically couldn't bring myself to the studio. I didn't have a car.

I'd sold everything after moving back from Los Angeles. I preferred not to think of it as a failure. Instead of a walk of shame, I viewed it as a stride of pride. After all, who wants to waltz into the cemetery on their deathbed all intact and beautiful? I was more of the belief that skidding in all torn up, a little bit worse for the wear, was worth the stories behind the scars. That was a quote somewhere, for sure.

But those scars came at a cost, and this time, it was a car. As I walked down the lonely street, I forced myself to focus on the one piece of worth I had left in my life. The car, the costumes, the furniture, the computers had all been sold. But my grandmother's old farmhouse remained in my name. She'd died six months before and left it to me, and I was just coming back now.

On the market, it was worth next to nothing. *Location, location, location*, they said. Well, its location was crap. It was next to a small pond, just outside of Little Lake proper, not quite far enough to be a "private" farm but not close enough to be "in town." The place was old and borderline kept up enough to be livable, but nothing to brag about.

However, I loved it. The pale yellow house was built of character and smelled lightly of peppermint and honey. The floors creaked in all the familiar places, and the ceilings were tall and lofty. Every afternoon sunlight streamed into the huge, cobwebby windows, painting the floor in a golden glow, perfect for reading a book on the couch. More importantly, it reminded me of my grandma. And, it was mine.

A car honk pulled me out of my reverie. I had about two miles left of a hike to get home, a walk I didn't mind. It'd give me something to keep my mind off the murder, get me some exercise, and take up some time. All for the price of zero dollars.

But as I continued down the side of the road, visions of Anthony Jenkins kept coming into my mind. I'd seen him on a few occasions, and even talked to him on the phone before I'd moved from California. But there had been nothing between us. Nothing at all.

I'd paid him my rent. We'd had a bargain—I had no incentive to kill him. And despite him being a little bit creepy, I couldn't see a reason anyone else would want to kill him either. He was a staple in town—a strange man with greasy hair who was harmless. Every town had one of them.

A rush of sadness coursed through my veins. Death was always a sad event, and it irked me beyond belief that people who knew me—had *known* me since high school—thought I was capable of being involved in something so dark. That's what really bothered me.

"Misty May?" A shrill voice pierced my eardrums.

I looked up. "I'd recognize that voice *anywhere!*"

The car stopped in the middle of Main Street, a minivan that stretched just under a block in length. The woman leaping out of the car was all cute and bubbly, short blonde hair kept in a perfectly coiffed soccer-mom bob.

"Misty May, how have you not stopped over yet?" Donna Bartman, née Adams, gathered me in a squeeze. She was a little cushier than during our high-school-days hugs, but I guess that was expected five kids later.

She was just as pretty and full of life as she'd always been. And as it always had been, we lived polar opposite lifestyles—perfect complements to one another. Her days revolved around family and kids, and activities and schedules. Mine varied erratically, leaving me feeling as if I was on top of the world one day and down in the dumps the next. A lot of people would call it unstable. I would agree.

"I've been back only a short time, and with the studio being built...plus, I heard you've been out of town?" I held my lifelong best friend at an arm's length, faux scanning her up and down. "Don, you look *great*."

"Thanks! I've lost thirteen pounds since baby *numero cinco*. We've been visiting Nathan's family up in the Cities for the past couple weeks before the kids start school again, and we just got back last night." She paused, her breath coming in short gulps. "How are you?"

Her question struck a chord deep inside. It suddenly seemed like it'd been a long time since anyone had asked me that question and meant it. I'd moved across the country, poured my heart into a new business that was on the verge of failing, and been accused of killing a man, but it was this simple question that caused my eyes to well up with tears.

"I'm okay," I said, my voice cracking. I sat down on the curb, right there on Main Street, and let the tears peppering my eyes skid down my cheeks.

Donna didn't miss a beat. She just plopped right next to me and threw her arm around me, rubbing my back lightly as she'd done numerous times before: after the first night we'd discovered wine and decided to drink *all* of it, when we'd gotten in trouble for breaking curfew, when we'd cried over unreturned phone calls from boys in fifth grade. I felt home for the first time since I'd been back.

"What's wrong?"

My lip quivered, and I prayed silently that neither Jax nor Alfred would drive by and see me weeping on the side of the road. Then again, Donna was Jax's sister, and she'd ream him a new one if she knew he was the reason for my tears.

The day's events poured out in uneven glops. My retelling of the story was all over the place, sprinkled with tidbits of my reasons for moving back from the City of Angels, the struggles of building a studio and adjusting to small-town life, and the reality of failing with my roster of zero students. How she managed to piece together my phrases into a coherent story was pure and utter magic.

"Wowzers, life is never boring around you, is it?" Donna put her arm around my shoulder. "The most exciting part of my day was when Nathan Jr. pooped on the potty."

"You don't want *this* kind of exciting," I sniffled.

"Look at the bright side," she said. "You didn't do it, right?"

"Right."

"Exactly. So find out who did, and you're golden."

"Find out who...you mean, like a detective?" I raised my eyebrows. "Isn't that what the police are for?"

Donna smirked. "Yeah, yeah, but they got a lot on their plates. Like enforcing the lawn-watering rules and making sure Bonnie Mayweather's dog doesn't crap on the fire hydrants."

She leaned forward. "Misty, let's make it happen. I'll help you. I could use a little excitement in my life."

I looked up. "I don't want to get you involved. You have a family, and I'm sure Nathan wouldn't approve."

"We won't do anything dangerous," she said. "Just poke our noses around a bit."

I shifted. "How do you mean?"

A slow smile spread across Donna's face. "I do have one piece of news to tell you, and I think it'll be *perfect* to help you figure out who knew Anthony Jenkins."

"Tell me!" I said, leaning forward. My eyes were now dry, an effect Donna always had on me.

"I'm taking over Sweets Candy Store! We'll be business neighbors!"

"That is amazing!" I said, squeezing my bestie into a bear hug. "Congratulations."

"Thank you," she said grinning. "And it will be perfect. People come to gossip in Sweets all the time. I have to kick Bonnie Mayweather out at store close three nights a week. She goes through a bag of jelly beans a day just to hear the latest news. I am sure Anthony will be the talk of the store over the next few weeks. I'll be able to poke my nose around a bit."

My lips quirked upward. "That would be so great, Donna. Wow. Thank you so much."

Donna nodded. "Of course. I *have* to show you what I've done with the place. I hate to toot my own horn, but I really love the new setup."

Sweets, the rusty town candy store, had been around ever since my parents were born. There was an old-fashioned soda fountain, a counter full of enough ice cream to give you a brain freeze for years, and so much sugar your teeth decayed a little bit every time you walked into the store. It was glorious.

"I'm thrilled that you've found something you want to do," I said. "I don't know how you manage your time. Are you Superwoman?"

She shifted, uncomfortable as usual with a direct compliment. In addition to being awesome in all sorts of ways, she was also humble. But as soon as Donna resumed talking about her new business, the sheen returned to her eyes, and her voice sizzled with life. "I can do it part time when the kids are in school and have the high school students help out in the other seasons. It'll keep me busy—plus it's good for the town. They were gonna shut it down. But anyway, more about that later. Right now, we gotta focus on getting you out of this mess."

"How do you figure we do that?"

Donna shrugged. "Well, if it wasn't you, then it's gotta be somebody else. We could start by trying to figure out who might've wanted Anthony Jenkins dead."

"Or at least what he was doing in the alley behind my studio, or who else was around on Wednesday," I said thoughtfully. "But it's been so long since I've been back in town, I can't think of who Anthony might've had a beef with recently."

"Good thing you have me on your team then," Donna said with a wink. "Like I said, Sweets is great for gossip!"

"By the smile on your face, I'm guessing you have an idea where we could start?"

"I would suggest starting with his wife," Donna said, looking at her watch.

"So soon? Do you think she'll want to talk about her husband's murder already?"

"Mr. and Mrs. Jenkins had a very unique relationship," Donna said slowly. "Strained might be the word to describe it. Let's see if she's open to us stopping by. If not, we'll leave."

"I don't know what I'd do without you," I said, leaning in toward my friend and nudging her gratefully. "You're one of the main reasons I moved back."

"Little Lake's not the same without you," Donna said happily. "I'm glad you're back."

A decent line of cars had built up behind Donna's ginormous van on Main Street. There was plenty of space for them to go around, but Little Lake was full of the nosy type of citizens, small-town folk who loved to gossip. Seeing me have a breakdown on the side of the road would be the beauty parlor equivalent of obtaining a front-page scoop. They'd be rich in gossip for the week.

"You'd better go," I said. "Thanks again."

"Call me!" Donna said as she waved at all the cars and took a small bow. "I want to help you with this thing."

The drivers honked and hooted and catcalled, most of them over seventy years old.

"I will," I said, gesturing for her to get in the vehicle.

"Hey, why are you walking, anyway?" Donna asked.

"No car." I shrugged.

"You got food?" she asked.

"Froot Loops."

"Get in."

CHAPTER FOUR

————

"How's your love life?" Donna glanced over a Spider-Man water bottle, a ratty teddy bear, and half a pack of Twizzlers to where I was perched in the minivan's passenger seat.

I stretched one leg on the dash, just like I used to in high school when we "borrowed" her parents' car for football games.

I gave her a *look*. "I've given up."

"I'm sure it's not *that* bad. At least you have funny stories about crazy dates. I live vicariously through your tales. What about that latest guy you were seeing?"

"What guy?" I crossed my arms. "My story well has run dry recently. I've given up. Too depressing. I've gone out with actors and models who think they're successful, bankers who think they're funny, and account managers who think they're interesting. Nothin'. I can't seem to catch a break."

"Well, maybe now that you're back..." Donna trailed off. We both knew that everyone worth having was already taken. According to Little Lake, my prime marrying years had been wasted on expensive, meaningless dates: guys who didn't call when I wanted them to and others who called too often when I didn't want them to.

"Now that I'm back, what?" I sighed. "Donna, don't start. I'm not looking for a date."

"Just curious," she said. "How'd things go with Jax, by the way? I heard you two had a run-in."

I could tell she was trying for casual. Her eyebrows knitted with concentration, and her voice threaded with hope. It didn't work—I could tell she was listening closely for my response.

"Besides the fact that the only reason he stopped to talk was to bring me in for questioning?" I asked, heavy on the sarcasm. "It went wonderfully. Why do you ask?"

"No reason," she said, glancing at her nails as they tapped the steering wheel. "He's actually dating right now." She flicked her right blinker up. "I don't like her, though. Prissy *b* word."

"Mm-hmm. Interesting." I pointed out the window. "Hey, doesn't Anthony's wife live over that way?"

"She does." A small smile quirked at Donna's lips as she pulled a U-turn. "I guess if you're not bringing dating stories to the table...we'll have to create our own entertainment."

I cracked a grin. "You don't have to help, Donna. I just want to chat with his wife for a minute and see if she has any idea why Anthony might've been near my studio, see her reaction of who might want him dead. Maybe he had a meeting at the building with another tenant. And if so, I want to find out exactly *which* tenant that might be."

"I know you find it difficult to ask for help, Misty," Donna said. "So let me put it this way. Nathan and I have been married for ten years. I love the man, but I could use a little extra adventure outside of dirty diapers and spit-up. Besides, don't secret agents get to have cocktails every once in a while?"

"Is Froggy's open?" I asked, realizing my stomach was growling quite loudly. "I want to get to Anthony Jenkins's place, but I haven't eaten all day, and the adrenaline took a lot out of me. Maybe a quick burger first?"

"Of course Froggy's is still open. Mr. Olsen refuses to die. He's preserved by vodka, a little bit of piss 'n' vinegar, and lots of nasty words." Donna clicked her nails on the steering wheel. "Burger and martini time?"

"Don't you have to get the kids?"

"They're at Gram and Gramps for the night. Nathan's picking them up tomorrow morning after his shift. I have time for a quick bite to eat. Then Mrs. Jenkins. I can't imagine she'd be out and about today, with what's happened. The town would swarm her for gossip. She'll be tucked inside her home."

"I just hope she doesn't mind a little company," I said softly. "Because I really need some answers."

* * *

"You're back, eh?" Mr. Olsen croaked, the oldest man in the universe, or so it seemed. He'd been ninety since I was born. "I remember ye."

"Really?" I raised my eyebrows. "I've changed a bit."

Mr. Olsen eyed up colorful hair, which was usually a dirty brown, some days blondish, currently with blushing-pink and lusty-lavender ombré tips. I had a tattoo around one shoulder, clearly visible under my stretchy leotard top, and then there were the fishnet stockings, but I didn't think he could see those under my sweats.

He scooted up a pair of antique reading glasses onto his wrinkled face, white whiskers sprouting from orifices I didn't know could sprout hair. "I see ye have. Takin' ye clothes off for money out in that city of Caley-fornia."

"California is a state these days." I leaned against the counter. "And I'm a burlesque dancer, *not* a stripper."

"Don't you be bringing that back to Little Lake, corrupting all the young minds."

"I'm offering classes to those over the age of eighteen." I tapped my fingers. "Can I get a very dirty martini and a very large hamburger?"

"Jax was in here asking about you this morning." Mr. Olsen wiped a glass down, his eyes on me. I guess years of experience made the man capable of moving around the bar like a ballerina. I would've knocked over six glasses and a fifth of vodka by now, but I bet he hadn't broken a glass in over sixty years.

"About what?" I looked at Donna. Her lips were pursed in a tight line as her eyes scanned the numerous choices of booze behind the bar. As a busy mom, probably she didn't get out much.

"Double my order please," I said. We'd be here all day if I let Donna decide. "Mr. Olsen, what was he asking about?"

"He wanted to know if yer was a good egg." Mr. Olsen poured some olive juice straight from the carton into what looked like a jug of vodka.

"What'd you tell him?"

"You'z a troublemaker. Cow tippin', high school boozin', purple hair, and tattoos who knows where, takin' off clothes for money...nah. He could do better."

"I appreciate the honesty." I took two huge martinis, one with extra olives. I smiled. "You remembered. I like a million olives."

Mr. Olsen grunted. I think that was maybe a sign of affection. "Here's your burger. Maybe you have some potential..."

I winked at Donna as he mumbled away about rainbow hair and "fishing line" stockings ruining a girl's image.

"Bottoms up?" Donna extended her arm and hooked an elbow around mine, and together we downed our martinis in one gulp.

"You feeling like a spy?" I asked.

"Probably we should have one more," she said.

"Probably you're right."

* * *

Giggly and a little bit tipsy, we walked down the sidewalk and made our way slowly up the steps of the now-widowed Mrs. Jenkins's house.

"Are you all right?" I whispered a bit loudly.

Donna shrieked her response, throwing her arms wide. "I haven't had a martini since kid numero four. I feel alive!"

I belatedly put a hand over her mouth, but it didn't stifle a thing.

The front door was whisked open by none other than the widow herself, a cigarette dangling from plum-colored lips, her toes separated by those pedicure doohickeys, and a bathrobe half open, exposing a small lacey bra and granny panties.

"Whadda ya doin' here?" Mrs. Jenkins rasped. "Donna? What the hell? I'm a widow. People is supposed to be leaving me alone. But *no*. They're bringing all sorts of pies and lasagnas and crap like that. How'm I supposed to keep this figure with all that food?"

I cleared my throat. Mrs. Jenkins was forty-nine going on eighty-four, having tanned about a hundred times too many in her teens. Her skin put her in the same class as an elephant, and her hair was as fried as a chunk of hay.

"Well, we didn't bring any food—don't worry." I thought wildly about what might get us through that door.

Donna, meanwhile, took a step and started to speak but got distracted and stumbled, her right foot coming down a little too far off the side of the cement stairs leading up to the front door. She face-planted beautifully into the rose bushes, her arms flailing, hair splayed like a spiderweb between the thorns.

"Are you *drunk*?" Mrs. Jenkins asked.

I extended a hand to Donna, but an idea popped into my head, and I looked behind Mrs. Jenkins hoping for a glance of her kitchen. I was rewarded with a perfect view of a liquor cabinet, more than a single person's supply of wine and a wide variety of the hard stuff.

I patted Donna on the back and met Mrs. Jenkins's gaze. "I brought you a drinking buddy."

Donna pulled herself up, nearly toppling me right over with her in the process. Thankfully, she caught on quickly. It was possible the fall had shaken some *sober* into her.

"Yep. We thought you might want a swig of vodka, and a girl knows it ain't classy to drink alone," Donna said.

Mrs. Jenkins's eyes scanned us skeptically for a brief second.

I took a deep breath, my mind fighting through the alcohol fog to appear as coherent as possible.

"You gals drink tequila?" Mrs. Jenkins flicked her ashes onto the front steps, barely missing my toes.

"Heck yeah." I'd drink anything that got me some questions answered. Plus, for all I knew, I was headed to jail soon—I should probably drink as much tequila as I could while I was still a free bird.

Mrs. Jenkins turned and walked inside her smoke-filled home. It was dusty, rusty, and all sorts of unorganized. I covered my mouth in an attempt to neither cough nor snort as our hostess led us to the kitchen like an awkward duck, thanks to her pedicure toe doodads.

"I don't got limes. There's a shortage in Mexico, thanks to those drug dealers, so I can't afford them. Salt is in those McDonald's packets by the sink."

I retrieved three packets as Jenkins poured three double shots. We poured the salt on our hands, licked it off, and downed the shots like we were twenty-one again. Except now it burned much worse, and I could already feel the start of a hangover.

Jenkins smacked her lips. "So whaddya really want?"

I stared at her blankly. "What do you mean? We came to pay our respects."

"Ain't nobody *respectin'* my husband. He wasn't a man to be respected, and that's just the facts."

"Well, he was my landlord, and I wanted to express my condolences." I rubbed my forehead as the tequila shot straight into my brain.

"Were you sleepin' with him?" She stared at me with beady eyes.

"What? No!" My eyes probably bugged out of my head. "I mean, no offense, Anthony's just...not my type."

Anthony had been a notch above unattractive in the greasy way a struggling used-car salesman might look almost presentable. He was creepy, morally loose, and a cheater in multiple senses of the word. I'd dated my fair share of fixer-uppers, even one with a unibrow, but I liked to think I retained *some* standards.

Jenkins took another shot and crossed her arms. "Yeah, you too pretty, I believe ya. But I tell ya, he was cheatin' on me with someone. I just don't know who."

Donna gave me an obvious stare. It was a good thing Jenkins was too busy lighting another cigarette and missed it completely.

"Any idea who it might be?" I asked.

"Who wants to know?" She blew a perfect ring of smoke right into my face.

I admired it for a long moment before responding. "Me."

"Why do you care?"

"Just curious. You don't have to answer." I shrugged and poured another shot. Like most citizens of Little Lake, Mrs.

Jenkins thrived on gossip. Maybe a dose of reverse psychology would get her talking.

I handed the round out. I raised my glass. "To Anthony."

Mrs. Jenkins snorted. The three of us clinked glasses. I downed about half mine and dumped the rest over my shoulder into the sink.

"So, are you doing okay?" Donna asked, putting a hand on Jenkins's shoulder.

"I'm fine." She shifted. Something in her body language suggested she wanted to talk but was still skeptical. "House will be quieter without him around."

Donna made a clucking sound in her throat. I think it was one of those noises that came with being a mother. My mom had made similar soothing noises when I was upset.

"No, no. That's a good thing." Jenkins looked out the window. "I like quiet. Prefer it, even."

Lost in a daydream, Jenkins blew out a few more rings of smoke. Donna and I looked at each other, and a prickling crept down the back of my neck. The nonchalance with which Jenkins spoke was eerie, as if she rather preferred her husband permanently silenced. She suddenly grabbed a lemon from the ledge above the kitchen sink, slapped it onto the counter, and slashed through it with a very large knife.

"I think we should probably get going." I jerked my head in the direction of the door.

Donna was eyeing the bottle of tequila again and didn't notice.

I cleared my throat.

An icy palm gripped my wrist. It felt like a frozen, nicotine-riddled skeleton clinging to my arm, and I shivered on reflex.

Jenkins leaned forward, her smoky breath oozing over my face, frying several of my nose hairs. "It wasn't me who kill't him."

The ugly, scary-looking butcher knife dangled from her other bony hand. The words I wanted to say got lost somewhere around my navel. Out of the corner of my eye, I caught Donna watching the exchange with a horrified expression, a bottle of tequila in one hand, a salt packet in the other.

"Uh…" I tried to pull my arm away, but Jenkins's grip cinched tighter. The nerve endings in my spine were firing away, sending tingles all across my nervous system. Even my scalp prickled.

"As much as I hated the man, I wouldn't've kill't 'im." She turned and spat a glob of disgusting black goop into the sink. "He waren't worth goin' to jail over."

"Do—do you know who might've killed him?" I eyed the knife warily, but Jenkins showed no signs of setting it down voluntarily.

"Tell me why you care so much."

"I…the police think I killed him." I watched the knife carefully. "But I didn't, I swear."

"I'd give yer a medal if you did, but I don't believe it." Jenkins's hand crept up my arm, and she had a boa constrictor effect on my bicep. "You wanna find your killer—find out who was sleepin' with him."

"Where would I start?"

Jenkins bit her lip. "He didn't talk to me. But he went out at night. Late, late nights."

"What was he doing?"

"Hell if I know." In one swoop, Jenkins dropped my arm and continued slashing through the lemon. "Like I said. He didn't talk to me."

Donna set down the tequila bottle and gazed around the kitchen. "Do you mind if we take a quick glance around, see if there's anything here?"

Jenkins was more occupied with the lemon than anything else at the moment. "Look at whatever yer want. He didn't come here much 'cept for a few hours of shut-eye now and again."

I followed Donna out of the kitchen.

"I thought she was gonna stab you in the guts," Donna whispered. "You got lucky back there."

"I think we should leave," I said. "I'll take jail over a coffin any day."

"Quick glance, then we're out," Donna hissed. "Check it out."

Donna pointed toward what appeared to be a bedroom. There were mounds of clothes on a mattress in the corner, a few empty cages with what may or may not have been animal remnants in the other corner, and a computer from the DOS era lopsided on a desk. The only thing in some semblance of order was a stack of comic books.

"His or hers?" Donna asked.

"I don't think she's spending her time reading books," I said. "She's more of a 'learn by doing' type, if I had to guess."

Donna cracked a smile. Very daintily she thumbed through a few books. She let out a low whistle.

Tucked inside the cover of one of the comic books was an old Polaroid of a much-younger Mrs. Jenkins in a very compromising position.

"That's actually pretty impressive." I cocked my head sideways. "I'm not sure how she got her leg like that."

A noise in the door startled both of us. Donna let the comic book fall back to the desk, and I whirled in a circle. With painfully slow velocity, the Polaroid of Jenkins swirled like a raspy old leaf in late fall down to the floor.

I raised my eyes after an eternity and met Jenkins's gaze.

She held the knife in one hand and a shot glass in the other. "I think it's time for you to go."

"We were just leaving." I took a step sideways, but neither Donna nor I moved toward the scary knife blocking the door.

"I was hot, wasn't I?" Jenkins asked to nobody in particular. She bent over and picked up the photo, examining it. "I *tried* to keep in good shape. I kept my skin tan, my nails painted, and my body hair contained. But it wasn't enough. Maybe if I looked younger, we wouldn't be having this little issue."

"Issue?" I crossed my arms and stepped back. "Are you talking about Anthony's death?"

Jenkins pursed her scaly lips. "That...among other things."

I looked at Donna, wondering if Jenkins was referring to the so-called illicit lover she'd suspected her husband of keeping on the side. Donna widened her eyes in response.

"Feel free to call us if you need anything…another drinking buddy or something." I spoke directly to the knife. "We should get going now. Donna's got kids at home."

"Five of 'em," she said quickly. "They'd do terribly without a mother."

I refrained from closing my eyes in exasperation.

Jenkins breathed out quickly through her nose and stepped out of the doorway, arms spread wide as if daring us to pass her. The knife pointed the way to the kitchen door.

I glanced at Donna, subtly sending my last words into her brain. I hoped she'd still be able to read my mind even after all our time spent apart in recent years. And even if she couldn't, it'd work out okay. Probably Donna could craft better last words for me than I ever could. All that was running through my brain at the moment was "uh-oh." And I'd prefer a more eloquent phrase on my tombstone.

After a hesitant step forward, I made a break for it. Four quick strides later and a heavily sucked-in gut, I felt as successful as if I'd been a knight who'd managed to slip past the dragon guarding the booty. Except in this case, the booty was my own, and it was in a beeline straight for the front door, Donna trailing closely behind.

"Thanks for the drinks, Mrs. Jenkins," Donna called, waving over her shoulder as we half jogged, half power walked down the front stairs.

"You're too perfect," I said to my friend. "You even remember to thank the hostess after she threatens us with a knife."

"Product of a small Minnesotan town," Donna huffed. "Manners. But criminy, I'm out of shape."

I was breathing pretty heavily too. We'd picked up our pace once we were out of sight of the house, neither of us wanting to be the first to slow down.

"Probably we're dehydrated," Donna said. "Walk to Froggy's, then take a drink break?"

"Abso-frickin-lutely. We can call a cab from there."

"What is this, Los Angeles?" Donna asked. We stopped running. "Here in Little Lake, you call your friends, not a cab. I'll have Nathan give us a ride back in the fire truck. I still get a little rush when I see him in his uniform."

"Too much information."

"Deal with it."

"You're back?" Mr. Olsen greeted us as we hauled ourselves into the bar.

"Martinis, please," I breathed.

"And a ride," Donna said. "Please."

He picked up the phone and punched 9-1-1.

We heard Lana, the dispatcher, ask in a nasally voice. "Is this an emergency?"

"No." I waved my arms at Mr. Olsen. "Not 9-1-1 worthy. Hang up."

"Yes, it is an emergency." Mr. Olsen glared at us, speaking into the phone. "Lana, darlin', I need help. I got two troublemakers in my bar. Send Nathan to pick up his wife."

CHAPTER FIVE

"Get out." Mr. Olsen shooed us out of the bar.

As tough as the old man seemed, I caught him watching from the front door of the bar until we reached Nathan's car. Bummer it wasn't the fire truck.

I tossed Mr. Olsen a jolly wave. He grunted and turned around, disappearing into the bar.

Donna was already in the car by the time I reached the vehicle. When I saw the driver, I jolted backward in surprise. "You're not Nathan."

"Nathan has better things to do than pick up two drunkies at one in the morning." Jax gave a half a smile and gestured for me to climb in. Since Donna had apparently called shotgun, I heaved myself into the backseat. I only tipped over once, which was impressive considering the martini count in my stomach.

"What could Nathan possibly have to do that's better than picking us up?" I glanced out the window. It was pretty neat—I could see stars here. It'd been a while. The City of Angels was named ironically, as it was far too lit up to see a shooting star, let alone an angel or a UFO.

"Fight fires." Jax clicked the blinker on.

"Please," Donna said. I could feel her eye-roll from the backseat. "The only fire he's putting out tonight is the one he's using to roast s'mores. I didn't hear a single call come through on the radio. Not so much as a toaster flamin' tonight."

"You wanted to check in on me, didn't you?" I interrupted, pointing at Jax. "Well, it's fine. I'm not going anywhere."

"You'd better not," Jax said.

I opened my mouth, but Donna reached into the backseat and put her hand on my knee. "Jax, you really don't think she did it, do you?"

I kept my gaze fixed out the window, but I was dying to know the answer as well.

Jax remained silent as he pulled into Donna's driveway.

He started to respond, but the long, pregnant hesitation was all I needed to hear.

"I'm going to walk home." I pushed the door open and slammed it violently.

"Wait, Misty," Donna called. "Let me drive you home. Of course you didn't do it. Jax is just trying to do his job."

"He's doing a great job of it. No bias whatsoever—it's like I'm a stranger." I wished immediately I could take back my short words, but I was drunk and tired and crabby and angsty and stressed and a bazillion other things, and Jax's pause had been the final straw.

"Mist..." Donna stopped walking. "Please don't go. Don't run away again. You just got back."

I turned around and slowed to a stop. "I'm sorry, Donna. I really appreciate everything you've done for me—coming with me tonight, offering to help. I'm going to figure this out. I'm not gonna run away."

She smiled. "Good. I'm here if you need."

I gave her a smile. "I'm going to walk home though. I need some air."

"No problem. Call if you need."

"I will." I gave her a quick wave but I didn't tell her two important details. The first, I didn't have a phone. My cell had been shut off courtesy of overdue payments after my money disappeared into the studio.

The second problem was that I couldn't promise not to run away. I'd been running most of my adult life, and it was the easiest solution. It'd helped me avoid plenty of problems thus far. I was invested in Little Lake only because of my studio. And my family. But if the studio didn't work out...how on earth could I afford to stay in Little Lake?

I kicked the dirt on the side of the road as I walked. I only had a mile or so to go, and it was a pleasant fall night. The evening had been gorgeous and cool, the leaves changing into beautiful golden shades and pumpkin orange colors. The scent of mulled wine and Honeycrisp apples floated lazily across the fields from the giant orchard on the outskirts of town. The middle of the night turned crisp and chilly, but there was something invigorating about the fresh fall temperatures. If things were different, I could see myself settling down in Little Lake.

Except things weren't different, and the sad realization that very few people would miss me if I left hit me hard in the gut. I took a seat on the curb and let a few gigantic tears creep from the corners of my eyes.

Donna would miss me, and my nine-year-old sister. The latter was a large reason I'd come back to my grandmother's house in the first place. It was hard to take her to movies and help with homework from three thousand miles away.

The rest of my family was a bit preoccupied and wouldn't exactly notice my absence: Mom was in the middle of whirlwind marriage number six, Dad ignored the fact that I danced for a living, which left us very little to talk about, and the rest of my sisters were scattered throughout the state, busy with their own families.

And Jax—I'd be getting rid of a pain in his ass if I left town. I'd be doing him a favor by running away for the second time.

Speaking of the Little Lake Devil, Nathan's car cruised to a stop in front of me. I quickly wiped my eyes and stood up, brushing my hands on my pants.

"Go away," I said as Jax rolled the window down.

"No."

"Yes."

"No."

"Don't be a pain in my rear end," I said.

"Don't be a pain in *my* rear end."

"Why did you drive by?"

"Donna mentioned a crazed, drunken Mrs. Jenkins showed you her knife."

"So?"

"I don't want my main suspect dead."

"How romantic." I crossed my arms.

"Get in."

"No!"

"What if I told you that you're not the only suspect?"

I took a step forward. "What?"

Jax sighed. "You're our main suspect, but there're others. I shouldn't be telling you this. But if you *didn't* do it like you say, then you have to be careful because there's a killer out there."

I leaned on the window, biting my lip. "Shouldn't you be scared of me then, if you're so convinced I'm the killer?"

"Honey, I've never had a problem pinning you down."

I bit back a remark and resumed walking down the side of the road. It was driving me up a wall how some moments Jax was as playful as the day we'd fallen in love, and other moments he was asking me questions, appearing for all intents and purposes to believe I'd killed a man. If he was doing this to get back at me for my choices from ten years ago, it was more than working. And in my book, even a little unfair.

"I'm sorry." Jax eased the car into motion and matched my pace. "Please let me drop you off at home."

"No. Thank. You." I punctuated my words with a finger against his window. I remembered too late it was Nathan's car and felt a little bit bad about the finger smudges. But not that bad, since Nathan had chosen to roast s'mores instead of pick up his wife and me, which had prompted this whole situation in the first place.

"I'm following you home then."

"Fine. I'm not going to talk to you. Please don't run my toes over." I slowed my pace, hoping he'd get the picture and go home. At this rate, it'd take me an hour to get home.

"I got all night, hon. I'm clocking this as overtime. Staking out a suspect."

I showed him one finger that was particularly useful. The long one sandwiched between two shorter ones on either side. Then I wiggled it a little bit. I stomped at a snail's pace for a few minutes, but pretty soon I couldn't stand myself going so slowly, so I resumed normal human walking pace.

Jax coughed, rolled down both windows, and started blaring a *Rocky* theme song.

My ears burned a bit as "Eye of the Tiger" accompanied my nighttime walk of shame home, but I refused to dip my chin. In fact, the only time I faltered during the entire trip home was when Jax switched the radio to play the first song we'd danced to in high school. It'd also been the first song we'd made out to, and gone to second base to, and the first song we'd...well, you get the picture.

I stutter-stepped for a second when it came on but was proud I didn't allow myself to look back. By the time I got to my front door, I gave myself one tiny glance back out of the corner of my eye.

Jax waved as I let myself in the creaky old house, and I was relieved he was too far away to see the wetness pooling in my eyes for the ninetieth time that night. Boy, being home sure did a number on my internal sprinkler system. Hopefully by tomorrow the sinuses would be plumb cleared out.

* * *

The morning boasted a bright sun, a cheerful chirping coffee machine, and the promise of a perfect fall day along the Mississippi River. It was a day that begged for a run through crunchy leaves, a slice of pumpkin pie with extra whipped cream, vanilla ice cream, and a warm apple cider on the porch.

I took a deep breath and puttered around the house. I wasn't a particularly early riser on a normal day, but today I had a long list of things to accomplish, so I was happy to be up and at 'em early. I still had a long way to go in finding another suspect in Jenkins's murder, and sleeping the day away wouldn't get me anywhere.

For a brief moment this morning, I'd been able to put the events of yesterday behind me. For example, when I stretched out on my nice, clean sheets upon waking, going to jail had been the furthest thing on my mind. As I took my first glorious sip of coffee (with a boatload of milk), a relaxing day preparing my studio seemed more appropriate than getting a phone call from the police station.

But then the flash of excitement I'd felt seeing six notifications in my email about students wanting to sign up for burlesque classes brought me back to reality. It didn't take a genius to figure out the new students were probably just nosy citizens wanting to see what all the hubbub was about firsthand.

The word had gotten out by now about Mr. Jenkins's death. Between Mrs. Jenkins's loose tongue, Alfie's thrill of being on the case, and the sheer definition of small-town Little Lake life, secrets eased out during the darkness of night. And with the news of Anthony's death, the accusations around who dunnit would swirl closely behind, my name caught up in the whispered beauty-parlor gossip and quiet murmurings over a cold hard cider at Froggy's.

I groaned. Suddenly, the day didn't seem so promising. My coffee tasted significantly more bitter, and even my colorful Froot Loops looked dreary and sad, little o's floating in an ocean of milk that'd eventually sink them like the Titanic.

Maybe I was being a bit dramatic, but it wasn't every day I was accused of murder. I didn't know how to deal with these things.

I finished my coffee and slurped the sugary milk, the sweetness adding a little cheer back into my life. Grabbing another cup of coffee, I fumed over the responses I'd gotten to my burlesque class. Nobody—*nobody*—would touch my classes with a ten-foot pole for the entire time I'd been back.

Not until this morning, when I suddenly became the hottest piece of gossip on the town. Now everyone wanted front-row seats to the train wreck that was sure to erupt.

Well, I'd show them. Filled with sudden resolve, I downed my second cup of coffee, forgetting even to add creamer. I typed out an email to my new students:

Welcome!
~*An Intro to Burlesque*~
The Tease...
Welcome to the hottest, exciting new dance trend brought to Little Lake straight from the stages of LA. Your first sixty-minute session will feature some history, different styles, and the transformation of burlesque from its origin through today!
Then...

*We'll take it to the floor. You'll get teased with a variety of
burlesque styles: striptease, chair tricks, how to seduce with a
boa, sexy floor work, and a load of attitude.*
   Start time: 2:00 p.m. sharp
   *Attire: clothes you feel sexy enough to dance in
   (Please make sure you can move around!)*
   Where: the new studio next to Sweets
*I will supply boas (with sparkles to the lucky few), gloves, and an
oversize man's
nightshirt for everyone, in order to get the party started...
See you there!
Misty*

Before clicking "Send," I glanced over the six names I'd
compiled into a list. Barbara Jones—town busybody. PTA all-
star, chocolate chip cookie baker extraordinaire, soccer, hockey,
and softball mom all in one day, she had her pointy little nose in
everything.
   She appeared perfect from her shiny hair down to her
stair-stepped bottom, but I was willing to bet she couldn't
conjure up an ounce of sensuality if she tried. It'd be like
teaching a robot how to be sexy. However, she'd show up for one
session in order to get enough material to bad-talk me.
   I grumped for a moment, then moved on. Sarah
Sweeney—she was just on another planet entirely. Quiet and
reserved, I would never have guessed she'd sign up. We'd never
been friends, but she seemed sweet. There were two names I
didn't recognize, though it was possible they'd married and I
didn't recognize their last names.
   Then there were two surprises. If it was the Sarah
Richardson I suspected, she'd been my worst enemy in
kindergarten. She moved suddenly up to the big city for first
grade (i.e., a small suburb of Minneapolis, which at the time
seemed as exotic as Mars), and I'd hoped she'd been sucked into
the Mississippi River.
   Rumors had drifted around that she'd moved back while
I was out of town, though I had yet to run into her. Which was a
good thing, because I was still holding a grudge from the time
she stole my tooth out from under my pillow at a sleepover and

stuck it under hers for a dollar. A dollar bought a lot of gumballs back in those days.

My breath caught at the next surprise. The name loomed large and a little bit wobbly on my screen: Mrs. Jenkins.

This would be interesting.

I refused to let my mind wander to sinister thoughts, like if Mrs. Jenkins would try to strangle me with a feather boa or suffocate me with a man's button-down shirt. I definitely didn't think about whether or not she'd bring her knife with her, and the thought of calling the police only very briefly crossed my mind. But instead of focusing on the negatives, I tried to look at the silver lining.

At forty bucks a pop for the introductory class, I was headed straight for $240. Which was maybe more of a grayish cloud than the silver lining. When I said the number aloud, two hundred bucks didn't seem like a whole lot of money. But I could buy a good amount of Froot Loops with that dough. Or pay my cell phone bill. Hell, I'd even have a little left over for a lollipop at Sweets. Or even get started on my rent payment for next month.

Filled with these jolly thoughts, I attempted to whistle as I straightened my purple-and-pink-tipped hair. I hoisted on a fresh pair of shorty shorts and a clingy tank top, pulling on a skirt over the shorts. I had a few errands to run before class this afternoon, and there was no sense changing in a few hours. I applied a quick layer of mascara and some Peeps-flavored lip balm.

I'd show this town the art of the tease.

CHAPTER SIX

———

I threw a baggie of Froot Loops into my purse and filled up a bottle with tap water. No more fancy Santa Monica bottled water for me—I was a babe on a budget. I grabbed a light sweater and locked up my grandmother's house. *My house.* I wasn't sure if I wanted to get used to that idea or not. Owning a house here meant roots, payments, responsibility. All words that scared me more than a little.

Fueled by coffee and sugar, now was as good a time as ever to start looking for where Anthony Jenkins went out during his late-night escapades. The logical place to start was Sweets. I'd be able to kill not two but *three* birds with one stone: check out the studio and make sure it was free of crime scene debris, prep it for class, then swing by the candy store for advice. And maybe a lollipop. (Fine, four birds with one stone. I was in need of a lollipop to help with my hangover. Greasy food just didn't do the trick for me—I needed raw, pure sugar injections.)

The walk was pleasant and fast, and I arrived at the studio pretty much sweat free, except for a little bit of moisture on my lower back. I passed by Sweets and waved at Donna, signaling I'd be right back. On the way into the building, I nodded at a pretty blonde, probably on her way to a car parked in the lot behind the building. So far so good—no signs of a murder anywhere on the premises. I marched into the studio feeling fairly lighthearted that my baby was up for class. The floors shined, the lights shone clearly, and...

I stopped. The word *Killer* was written across the mirror in dark, shining red letters.

I took one step closer. Below it, in uneven cursive, was the phrase *Watch Your Back.*

My heart pounded. I glanced around the room, frozen. If the trespasser was still here, I didn't want to run into them. Not if they were mad enough to vandalize my property and threaten me all in one swoop.

I took a step back, glancing around the open studio and seeing nobody. But the reflection of the letters made me see red in more ways than one. A burning rage burst behind my eyes. There was only one closet in the place, and the rest of the studio could be seen by mirrors. If the culprit was here, I wasn't going to hide.

In three long strides, I reached the closet full of sexy playthings: satin gloves, button-down shirts, and rhinestone bras. Without thinking, I yanked the door open. A single black feather laced with sparkles drifted lazily to the ground.

I was alone.

"What happened here?" A raspy, familiar voice shattered the eerie silence behind me.

I spun around faster than I thought possible, and the feather caught a gust of wind and floated toward Mrs. Jenkins.

"Did you do this?" I asked.

"No, I didn't." Mrs. Jenkins walked unsteadily forward, glancing around the room. She bent and picked up the feather, running it lightly across her lips. The effect was a creepiness that caused tingles to scurry down my spine.

"Then what are you doing here?"

"I wanted to stop by the studio before our first class this afternoon." She fixed me with a nonchalant, even stare that caused me to wonder the level of this woman's sanity. "With my husband being murdered here and all, you'll understand that I had to deal with that alone."

I crossed my arms. "I have to call the police. It's probably best if we don't touch anything and wait outside."

We held each other's stare for a long while.

"Yes, you're right," she said finally, tucking the feather into the pocket of her skintight jeans. There were enough holes in her jeans that I wondered if she'd let a woodpecker loose on them. Her shirt was slightly more material than a bra, cropped to just below her chest and tight enough that I could see the outline of *everything* underneath. Each and every suntanned wrinkle.

I remembered with a crash of reality that I didn't have a phone. "I'm going to go wait in Sweets."

I left the room without a backward glance, hoping against hope that Mrs. Jenkins would leave as well. A part of me wanted her to stay in the studio so the cops could catch her red-handed and take her away. Sure, I wasn't sure if it was Mrs. Jenkins who graffitied my studio at all, but her whole demeanor freaked me out. The sight of her turned my stomach, and it wasn't just the poor choice of clothing or excessive amounts of skin on display.

I pushed open the door to the candy shop.

"Can I use your phone?" I asked. "I gotta call the police."

"For what now?" Donna handed over a light-pink fancy phone. Something I might've had back when I had enough money to live on.

"Someone wrote mean words in my studio. And I'm not sure whether it's blood or spray paint, but I'm not licking it to find out."

The phone rang once. I expected Lana to answer the emergency line.

Instead, I got a male voice. "Hey, baby, what's up? Thanks for the note in my lunch this morning...I don't know what got into you, but I'd *love* to cash in on that offer tonight—"

"Nathan," I interrupted. "This is Misty. Didn't I call 9-1-1?"

There was a long silence. I could feel Nathan's embarrassment from across the invisible phone line. "Oh."

"I didn't know 9-1-1 doubled as a dating hotline." My joke fell flat, and I cleared my throat. "But seriously, is this 9-1-1?"

"Yes. Lana recognizes Donna's number and patches it straight to me. We always got some emergency with the kids puking or pooping or expelling bodily fluids of some sort in a location they shouldn't."

"Ah. Well, I'm looking to report some stuff. Could you give me over to someone?" I glanced out of the corner of my eye at Donna. "Preferably not Jax."

"Sure. No problem. Here you go."

"Sorry about that." Lana, the ageless dispatcher, came back on the line. "I didn't realize...almost everyone has a cell these days."

"Yeah, well. Not this girl." I gave a weak smile at Donna, who was looking on curiously.

"I understand. How are you? It's been a while since you've been back...last time you weren't old enough to drink a beer." Lana cackled. "Though I don't ever recall that stopping you."

"Yes, yes. Good stuff. So, is there someone around I can talk to? Preferably—"

"Preferably not Jax, I'm guessing. You two had a bit of a falling out when you moved away, didn't you? What was that all about, anyway? I always thought you two kids were perfect for each other," Lana drawled.

"Things change," I said. "Distance is tough, you know. Anyway, if you could just..."

"Yes, of course. Say, how are you doing with the whole Mr. Jenkins thing? I personally don't think you could've ever done something as horrendous as that, but you know, the justice system doesn't work based on trust." She laughed until she coughed.

I sighed. "I appreciate your vote of confidence, Lana, but really...could you please?"

"Right. Right. I'll pass you along now."

"Howdy," Alfred sang over the line. "Howdy doody."

"Oh, great," I muttered. I held a hand over the phone and mouthed to Donna. "Seriously? It's *The Brady Bunch* over there."

Donna opened her eyes wide and nodded.

"Hi, Alfred," I said. "I'd like to report some vandalism."

Amid *hhhmmms* and sympathetic *awwwws*, Alfred listened until I was finished speaking.

"I'll be right over to check it out." Alfred paused. "Do you have any guesses who did it?"

I paused. "Mrs. Jenkins was around the studio when I found it. Other than that..."

Alfred cleared his throat. "I'm coming. Be over in a jiffy."

I hung up and handed the phone back to Donna, who was watching with large eyes. "Alfie still has that crush on you?"

"Watch it." I gave her squinty eyes. "I don't want to hear about it."

"Or else?" Donna handed me a Red Vine.

I took one large bite. "What did you have planned for Nathan tonight?"

Donna's cheeks turned red as my licorice, and all of a sudden she became very busy reloading the Jolly Ranchers.

"That's what I thought."

CHAPTER SEVEN

"Do you want the good news or the bad news first?" Alfred looked at me from across the studio.

I sighed. "Do they always come in pairs?"

"I'll start with the good." Alfred walked over. "It's not blood. It's a goopy paint."

"That's good. But I'm scared to hear the bad."

"You're in trouble." Alfred looked up at me.

"Funny, I came to that same conclusion yesterday. What else did you find out?"

He stretched upward and gave a feeble cough. "Well, the words say *Watch Your Back*."

"Yes. I can read."

"That means someone's out to get you. Any idea why?"

I shrugged. "I moved back to this godforsaken town to live in my grandmother's house and be closer to my baby sister. What on earth is offensive about that?"

"What about the whole...Mr. Jenkins thing?"

"I'm trying to figure that out! I already told you, I know nothing about him except he was my landlord. That's it. He had *no* reason that I can think of to be near my studio that day. I can't find anyone who has any idea."

Alfie nodded, scribbled a few notes onto a little pad he pulled from his pocket, and stepped back. "I'll have a few guys take some pictures and see if they can find anything."

"Thank you. I appreciate that."

"I doubt they'll find anything," Alfie said. "This looks sprayed on, and I'm nearly positive they wore gloves. I don't think we're dealing with an idiot here. We're talking about murder."

"Right," I said. "A murderer dislikes me, and I don't even know why."

"Do you have a safe place to stay?" Alfie asked.

He seemed genuinely concerned, which is the only reason I responded. "Yeah. I'm in my grandmother's old house."

"All alone?" Alfie asked. "Won't you be scared? If you need someone to swing by and make sure things are okay..."

"Alfie..."

"Too far." Alfie took a step back as I took a step forward, and unfortunately we had a minor collision.

He'd reached back to put his notebook away, but his hand accidentally brushed my butt en route to his pocket.

Great, I thought. *Now I gotta shower off Alfie germs, on top of evading a killer* and *proving my innocence*. What a great day this was shaping up to be.

* * *

"Nothing's going right today," I said to Donna as I leaned on the counter of Sweets.

"I don't envy you." She gave me another Red Vine. "Here's one for the road. Go for a run or something. Your class isn't until two, so you'll have plenty of time. It'll help you clear your head until your studio's all cleaned out. I called my janitors, and they'll clean it up for you. It'll be ready by your class this afternoon."

"You're the best." I gave Donna a hug. "You're the one reason I'm not already back in California. Well, that and the fact I might be arrested if I fled the state."

I chomped down a strand of licorice while heading to my small office at the end of the hallway outside my newly vandalized studio. I pushed open the door hesitantly.

I'd barely spent any time in the office to date. Most of my time had been spent in the studio, organizing props, polishing, scrubbing and cleaning, testing out the virgin floors still free of chair scratches. The office smelled like Lysol and fake flowers. Someone, probably Donna, had come in here after the crime scene crew had poked around and cleaned up.

There were flowers on the desk, and there wasn't an ounce of fingerprint dust anywhere. Someone had overdosed on the Febreze all over my chair from the smell of things, and my paperwork was more organized than when I'd put it there.

The faux clean scent started a wave of nausea that began in my semi-singed nostrils and trickled down to my gut. I quickly grabbed my running shoes from the bottom drawer of my file cabinets and turned to get going as fast as possible. I needed a distraction from thinking about Anthony's body tied in a pair of fishnet stockings, and a jog across town should tire me out.

One drawer caught my eye as I began to close my office door. It was slightly ajar, and there was a silvery-looking finger hanging out.

A glove finger, I told myself. *Relax.*

Pulling the drawer open, a full-length silver glove was half in and half out of a new package.

Hmmm. I had been saving these gloves for my first class and hadn't opened the package yet. I pulled the glove out and glanced over it quickly. The packaging had been torn, but the right glove was untouched in the wrapping. The left glove dangled haphazardly over the edge of the drawer.

"Ugh!" I let out a frustrated grunt. I'd been looking forward to one small luxury for my first class. New gloves. And the crime scene investigators had ruined even that. I felt a few angry tears building up, so I stashed the gloves back in the drawer, slammed it shut, and slipped on my running shoes.

I had to get out of here. Nothing felt clean. Nothing felt new. The joy that should've been cropping up for my first day of a new studio, new students, new classes was ruined. And not only was it not my fault, but I was being blamed for it. Why?

Why? The question pounded over and over in my mind as I set off down the pavement. I hadn't run in quite a while—not since I'd moved back, in fact. Fueled by the unfairness of it all, I felt ready to tackle a marathon. My feet carried me down the familiar road I'd run in high school.

It was a state trail running through the woods. Golden leaves fluttered around my shoulders, and orange, red, and yellow hues created a magical glow. I'd only ever felt compelled to bring one other person here with me. And it hadn't turned out well.

Memories of Jax and me strolling hand in hand during similar fall weather ten years before pushed out all grizzly thoughts of looming murder and danger. We'd been so in love. But I'd been stupid. So damn stupid, and by the time I'd tried to fix things, it'd been far too late. He'd moved on. And was still quite happily existing without me.

Why had I come back? There was nothing here for me except accusations of murder, threats to my safety, and a former lover I'd thought I was over, but wasn't...at least not according to the slivers of pain jolting through my core whenever Jax was around.

My pace quickened, breathing matching my faster strides. I hadn't run this fast in forever. I needed to be gone. To go away. To run.

I pulled up short at a small clearing, bent over in half, heaving as my guts burned and my breaths came in short, staccato bursts. The pain felt good. I took a few slow steps to catch my breath, gazing around the amazingly unchanged clearing.

A fallen tree trunk made a perfect bench along one side of the circular patch of dirt. All around, the trees cuddled in close, creating a cozy little fort where I'd come as a kid to gather my thoughts. I liked to think that the only other person to set foot here was...

I kicked aside some leaves and brushed a spot clean on the makeshift bench, plopping down unceremoniously. Charred remains of a decade-old bonfire pit littered the center circle, and I bet if I dug deep enough I could find a stolen beer bottle or box of cheap wine.

I'd been a straight A, overachieving student for most of my high school career. Not the obnoxious type, just the type who worked hard, didn't have a social life, and wanted to become the first female CEO of a bazillion dollar company. I'd been valedictorian and winner of the *Most Likely to Be Successful* banner at graduation.

The only fun I'd ever had was with Jax. Whatever had prompted him to notice a mousy, studious, absolutely average girl was beyond me. But once we'd started dating, he'd slowly begun pushing my buttons, helping me to lean on my rigid views of life. He'd given me my first beer, helped me achieve *drunk* for the first time, and kept me out past curfew. I pushed back, studying hard and vocalizing my need to get good grades and go to a good college, but little by little my self-imposed rules bent a bit and even broke on occasion.

He'd been the first (and arguably only) man I'd ever loved.

The night he told me he loved me, I'd had one thought: *if this isn't love, I don't know what love is. I don't want to know.*

My emotions had run so high: scared, thrilled, exhilarated—I'd cried out of happiness and sobbed out of fear that I'd lose him.

And when he asked me to marry him...

"Thought you might be here." The man himself stepped from the woods behind me, pulling a book of matches out of his pocket.

"What are you doing here?" I leapt up and took a few steps back. I didn't feel like getting surprised, scared, or arrested at the moment, and he'd already hit two of the three. I wanted to avoid the third.

Jax stepped past me, pushed away extra debris, and tossed a handful of twigs and leaves into the fire pit. He lit a match and tossed it onto the small teepee. It was ablaze in a second, a beautiful little fire. Looking around, he carefully selected a larger log and added it to the flames.

Watching him was a thrill in itself despite my desire to stay far, far away from the man I'd loved so hard. His naturally earned muscles rippled as he lifted another piece of wood, twisting his chiseled midsection and exposing a row of beauteous abs, visible through his tight, plain T-shirt. His hands, with a softness that I remembered so perfectly, gently placed the log on the pit and adjusted the fire as if his fingers contained magic. (Which they did—I can vouch for them. Pure wizardry, in fact). There was no other explanation for the feelings he could invoke through a single touch or a soft stroke.

My mind flickered through a reel of thoughts, none of which I could find the words to voice. He moved so easily, it seemed almost sacrilegious to break the flow with which he caressed the fire to a warm, sparkling life.

Appearing satisfied, Jax's gaze washed over me quickly, a question silent in his eyes. He looked away just as fast. A few short steps later, he perched next to me on the log.

"You're running." He stated a fact, didn't ask a question.

"No." I glanced down at my shoes. "Well, yes. But not far. Just...jogging."

"Right." The skepticism with which he spoke pained my stomach. It was as if he'd lost all faith in me.

I shook my head. I'd broken his trust, badly. I deserved it. I looked anywhere but him: up through the tree branches, deep into the fire, at each and every single twig and grass strand beneath my dirty running shoes.

I worked up the courage to look at him. "Look, I'm sorry. I'm sorry for what happened ten years ago."

Jax started to speak, but I put a hand up and spoke over him until he quieted.

"I should've apologized a long time ago. I tried but...well, I tried. But I didn't come back to take abuse for it."

"Why did you come back?"

It was my turn to pause. "Different reasons."

Jax let it drop. "Did you do it?"

"Do what?"

He leveled his gaze at me, and I knew he was speaking about Anthony Jenkins.

"Do you honestly think I did?" I met his gaze straight on. Neither of us wavered for a long moment. Eventually he looked away into the fire, and I followed suit.

"Tell me about the vandalism."

"What do you want to hear?" I watched the flames flicker red, blue, yellow. "Someone broke into my studio and painted a mess. I'm sure you've seen pictures."

He didn't disagree. "Did you do it?"

"I already...wait, the vandalism?"

Jax merely tipped his head downward as if not wanting to repeat his question.

"Why on earth would I?" My jaw hung open a bit. "You think I'd vandalize my own studio—a *brand new studio* that I poured my heart, soul, and every last penny into—with a threat to myself? For crying out loud, I'm so broke I eat Froot Loops for three meals a day."

"Not a healthy diet."

"Some people prefer their fruit in the form of a loop." I turned my nose up, dismissing his questions as the nonsense they were.

"You're a smart girl, Misty. I have no doubt you've already put together why I might suspect you did the vandalism. Nobody in their right mind would destroy something so important to their livelihood...unless they were trying desperately to avoid jail time. A few scribbled words on the wall beats a life in jail, eh?"

A bitterness welled up in my throat.

"The paint washes off, doesn't it?" Jax pressed.

It was too much. I couldn't handle this latest accusation. I leapt from the bench. "If you think I'm capable of murdering someone and vandalizing my own studio, then arrest me now."

My chest heaved as I looked down at Jax sitting quietly on the log.

I stuck my hands out front. "I'm sick of this. I can't stand it. Go ahead."

Jax stood and stepped toward me. I closed my eyes.

Instead of the cool clasp of handcuffs, Jax's warm, soft hands encircled my wrists.

"If you are as innocent as you say you are, then prove it." Jax pulled me close enough I could feel his breath trickle over my skin. Memories of nights huddled together in a one-person sleeping bag under the stars, cuddled up beside the lake, shrieking as we skinny-dipped under a brilliant moon rushed back.

"Tell me why I shouldn't go back to California. Get a job as a stripper. No paperwork there. It's what my life has come to, after all. Isn't it?" I pressed forward against him, my tone pleading. My lips were inches from his, begging to hear the words I wanted to hear. "It's what everyone here thinks of me anyway."

We stared into each other's eyes. He slid his gaze over my cheeks, down to my lips, and an uncontrollable shudder raced down my back.

Jax steadied me, his arms lightly resting on my shoulders. He brushed one index finger across my cheek. "No. Not me."

My gaze dropped, and I hoped he couldn't see the disbelief, relief, confusion—an entire spectrum of emotions—dancing across my eyes. Want and love were among them, I was sure of it.

I heaved a big sigh, gathered as much courage as I could, and offered a watery smile. "I don't know what to do besides disappear. I never thought I'd resort to becoming a stripper."

"So *that's* what you do," Jax said, his eyes crinkling in a smile. "I wondered."

I gave him a light slap on the shoulder. "Of course not. It's burlesque. It's the art of the tease—"

I tried to continue my explanation, but Jax pressed a finger to my lips. "Shhhh. Maybe you should give me a show, and I'll be the judge of that."

"Stop it," I said, laughing at his devilish grin. It was a miracle the man hadn't been swooped up and married by now. But then again, why would he be? He could charm the fishnet stockings off any girl. "You have a girlfriend."

Jax's smile faded slightly. "In all honesty, I've never known you to give up on something you want. No matter the cost."

His words sunk in slowly, bittersweet. In the past, the cost had been painfully high. I wasn't sure I could take risks that great again. I wasn't sure if it had been worth it the first time.

"Right now, I just want to teach my class in peace. And avoid life in prison. That'd be ideal."

Jax gave a smile, but it didn't make it to his eyes. "Then I'd say you want something pretty badly."

He took a few steps away before I could respond.

"Should I put the fire out?" I asked, for lack of better words.

"I'll give you some time to think. I'll be back in five minutes with some water. I parked not far away."

I nodded, feeling slightly numb all over.

"By the way..." Jax looked over his shoulder just before he disappeared between two trees. "What do you mean you tried to apologize?"

I glanced up, my mouth hanging unattractively open.

"Nothing." I shook my head. "Nothing. I didn't try hard enough."

Jax gave a singular nod, and this time he was the first one to disappear.

CHAPTER EIGHT

———

"Can we please, please, please go shooting on Friday?" A small human, who moved more like a bouncy ball than the nine-year-old girl she was, tugged on my arm. Though I hadn't lived in Minnesota since she'd been born, she'd been out to visit me in California a few times, and we Skyped once a week ever since she'd learned to use the computer. The distance hadn't kept us from developing a close relationship, and being home and able to see her in person was a thrill.

"We'll see." I planted my feet, trying not to topple onto her. My sister had gotten a brand new BB gun for her recent birthday, a gift from my brother who, of course, lived far enough away that he didn't have to deal with the ramifications of putting a metal gun in the hands of an elementary schoolkid. "Where's Mom?"

Harmony shrugged. "I don't know, but if we go shooting, can you please pick up more BBs? I ran out. Also targets. Mine are full of holes."

"Sure, Harmony." Unfortunately for her, my mother had decided to turn hippie right around the time my sister had been born. Before that, my mother had named my sister Aisling, a.k.a. "dream," during a brief gothic stint. My sister Charlie (real name Charles) got the worst of it during my mother's androgynous phase. All in all, the woman I called Mom changed men more quickly than I changed my hair color, and with it changed her *identity*.

I liked to say I went through a backward rebellion: my mom and dad had been unhappy together since I was born. I was the oldest. After two more children together and ten years, they divorced. My mom quickly began to "find herself," through process of elimination it seemed, and when gothic didn't pan out, she switched to hippie, and on and on went the cycle.

A few more children were added to the family throughout several additional phases. Going into high school, the only thing I wanted was normalcy. Hence the strict rules I set for myself and my no-nonsense policy toward anything out of the norm, unlawful, or subpar in terms of academic achievement. .

Now there were six of us kids, three from the same parents and three from my mom—and various partners. Harmony was the youngest, almost two decades my junior. She was part of the reason I felt obligated to come back and take over my grandmother's house. I knew how difficult life could be with my mother, and I wanted to be there when the going got tough. It wasn't saying very much that I considered myself a *normal* role model. But compared to my mother, I was as average as a very boring insurance salesman.

"There, there. Would you like a cup of tea? You seem stressed." Harmony dropped my wrist, which she'd been gripping tightly, and clamored over to the counter. Before I could respond, she had an array of teas set out and was filling the pot with water.

"I can do that." I stood. "Should you be using the stove?"

Harmony shot me a glance as if I were the most idiotic human being on the planet. "Of *course* I can use the stove. I'm *nine*."

The problem was, since I'd been back, I'd slowly been realizing that my sister had grown up into a self-sufficient young lady. I knew the feeling. When one grew up with a mom as flaky as ours, one learned to care for herself at a young age. It made me a tiny bit sad that my sister had spent nine years of her life becoming an independent little woman, and I'd missed a lot of it.

I reached out and squeezed her close. Harmony's small arms encircled my waist, and for a moment it felt like we were in our rightful places: She, a child in my arms. I, a responsible adult looking after my baby sis.

Then the tables turned and Harmony cast me a scolding glance. "Sit down and relax. Tell me about your day."

"When did you get so old?" I asked, sitting at the table and feeling like a child.

"I'm wise beyond my years." She giggled and winked at me.

"You're much wiser than me, that's for sure. And I bet you had a better day." I dunked my tea bag. "You know Alfred, the cop?"

Harmony wrinkled her nose.

"My thoughts exactly." I raised my eyebrows. "He touched my butt on accident today."

"Ewww! Gross. That's so sick." She squealed. "Boys are gross. I just want to be all alone like you when I grow up."

"Wow, gee. Thanks." I grimaced, not sure if that was the *healthiest* example to be setting for her. "Independence is good."

"All alone...who's all alone?" My mother breezed into the kitchen, tight yoga pants holding in her rather petite, almost fifty-year-old frame. She wore a strappy yoga shirt, bare feet, and a scrunchie. "No one's alone. We're all connected through this big, beautiful universe."

She scurried over to the refrigerator and pulled the door open. "Has anyone seen my yoga mat?"

"I bet it's not in there," I said, watching her sift through an array of yogurts.

"Hello to you too, darling." My mother waltzed over and kissed my cheek. "Don't you go spreading the nonsense that being alone is the way to spend your life. Just because you like to run away from—"

"I don't run away!" I stood up and took a few steps toward the front door. "What is it with everyone today?"

"There you go, dear, running away."

"I'm not running. I'm walking."

"You're walking very quickly," Harmony piped in.

I refrained from rolling my eyes at the world.

"Can you watch your sister Friday? I'm going out with Darren." My mom flounced down in the seat I'd recently evacuated.

"Who's Darren?"

"My yoga instructor." My mother leaned forward conspiratorially. "The only one in town."

"Wow, Mom. Good job." I eyed her up and down. That explained the getup.

"Do I look...yoga-ish to you?"

"Lose the scrunchie, Ma."

"I like the scrunchie."

"Darren won't like the scrunchie."

"But it's yoga-ish."

"No, it's hippie-ish."

"Oh." A little dejectedly, my mother pulled the scrunchie from her hair, which was still light brown and thick, curling in cute little swirls around her shoulder. Of all things to inherit from my mom, I wanted her hair. Instead, I'd gotten her average nose and nothing else. I'd also missed her ability to land an endless stream of dates, husbands, and friends. Despite being odd and flighty, my mother was a kindhearted fixture of the town.

She had friends from church, PTA, softball league, bar league baseball, and now yoga, I highly suspected, among a number of other things. My mom was pleasant and easy to get along with—as long as she wasn't your mother. Stability and discipline weren't high on my mother's priority list, which had made growing up under her quite a roller coaster.

"Friday is fine." I put a hand on Harmony's head. "We were gonna hang out anyway."

"Unless she's in *J-A-I-L*." Harmony spelled it out from under my hand.

I turned her head to face me. "Excuse me? Where did you hear that?"

"Honey, people are talking," my mother said. "I've gotten no less than eleven phone calls this morning."

"I didn't do anything!"

"Of course you didn't," my mother said. "We know that. It's just...people like to talk."

"What are they saying?"

Harmony opened her mouth to speak, but my mother shook her head. "I'm late for yoga class. Don't worry, dear. I'm sure everyone believes you didn't do it."

My mother whisked out the door, kissing both me and Harmony on the cheek but not quite making eye contact with me.

I gave a long, deep sigh.

"Life is tough sometimes, isn't it?" Harmony said.

"You're tellin' me."

"Here." My sister reached up and pulled down a box of Froot Loops. "This always helps me."

I smiled. "Guess we're related."

"Yeah." She grinned. "I'm glad you're back. It's not *everyone* who has an older sister that gets away with murder."

"I didn't do it!"

"I'm kidding. Lighten up, sista." Harmony shook her head, a smirk on her face as she popped in one Froot Loop after another.

"Gimme those." I ruffled her hair and grabbed a handful for myself.

"What's next?" she asked.

"I don't know. I have some more poking around to do, but I feel like I'm at a dead end right now. I need to find out what business Anthony Jenkins had in my office, but nobody seems to know."

"Maybe you're just not looking in the right spot. Sometimes if you take your mind off it, things just pop into your head. Like last night I was taking a shower, and the answer to my math homework just appeared right in my head."

"Are you trying to tell me I need a shower?" I asked.

Harmony grinned. "It's a saying. Just do whatever you do normally, and maybe something will come to you."

"You're smarter than most adults, you know that?" I raised an eyebrow at my sister.

"Yeah." She gave me a huge, cheesy smile. "I know that."

"And just as humble too." I grabbed my purse. "I've got a last errand to run before I teach class today. My first one."

"Don't forget about Friday," my sister called in a singsong voice.

"It's a date." I gave her a side hug and headed out the front door.

It'd be the only date I'd get in this town for a while.

Alfie's accidental butt graze excluded.

CHAPTER NINE

———

"Do you have any recommendations of what I should buy to shoot out of a BB gun?" I asked the robed man before me.

Father Olaf, the town pastor, opened a catalogue before him. "You're going to have to head over to Al's in order to get the good stuff."

"There's nothing here?" I looked around the lost and found at the church. I didn't make a habit of looting from the dredges of the parish, but Father Olaf was one of the best marksmen in town, and I thought he might have something left over he wouldn't need.

"I don't have anything here," he said, gesturing to the arrays of soccer balls, mittens, packs of gum, and the odd cell phone or two. "You better believe if someone dropped off a pack of BBs, I'd find a use for them."

"Okay, Al's it is," I said. "What should I be looking for?"

Father Olaf pointed toward the gun catalogue before him. He was not only the town pastor but also the head of Little Lake's social atmosphere. He ran the only Catholic church in town, and it was *the place to be* on Sunday mornings.

I wasn't particularly religious about going, but I'd been a member of the parish since I was a kid. Father Olaf had been there even longer than I had, though he appeared not to age. I think he might have been born sixty years old and would stay sixty years old until the end of time.

"This one is particularly dangerous," he was saying. "You'll want to be careful with those."

"Something less dangerous, maybe," I said. "We're just shooting for fun."

Due to Father Olaf's influence in the town, his church bulletin was the place for a business to be seen. I'd been begging to get an ad in there for my studio since I'd come back to town, but I'd been turned down time and time again.

"About the ad," I said, ignoring Father's explanation of why certain BB-gun bullets were particularly dangerous. "Can I please, *please* put an ad in the bulletin?"

He glanced at me with a fairly judgmental stare. Probably built up from years of practice in the confessional. "You didn't come here for advice on guns, did you?"

"Please," I begged. "Just one ad. It would really help."

He looked a bit disappointed, and I felt a twinge of guilt. It was true. I'd come here with an ulterior motive. My sister asking me to go shooting had been just the excuse I'd needed.

"You have no money for an ad. Plus, it's not a typical venture for the church to promote."

"It's a dance class. The citizens need something fun in their lives. Knitting club has plenty of ads and members already. Plus, I scheduled classes on a night that wouldn't interfere with Bible study."

"I said *no*."

My heart sank. "I need students."

"Then get them. But not through the church bulletin."

"Ugh..." My shoulders slumped. "Fine. But seriously, do you have a recommendation for a good shooting range? My sister is dying to go."

* * *

After meeting with Father Olaf, it was about time to head to the studio for class. Opening the door still felt a little bit creepy, even though the sun was shining, the sky a bubbly blue.

The building proved deserted upon a quick inspection. I set Harmony's BB gun down on the desk, ignoring the fact I'd held it in front of me like a real weapon as I quickly looked through my office and the studio for traces of life.

Luckily, not only was the studio free from creepy strangers, it was also free from red paint spelling out threatening words. Donna had made good on her word, and as I very quickly stuck my head in the office, I noticed she'd even set fresh sunflowers—my favorites—in a vase inside the room.

It smelled like a light mixture of false outdoors and fake wildflowers combined with Lysol and fresh-linen aerosol. The gesture was sweet, and I made a mental note to swing by Sweets and thank Donna for everything she'd done to get the place cleaned up in time for class.

I quickly grabbed a notebook from the desk and went back to the studio, where I plopped on the floor and started scratching down a few last-minute adjustments to my standard first-timer's lesson plan.

Today wasn't my first day teaching. When I'd lived in Los Angeles, I'd mostly been a performer, but I supplemented my income by teaching bachelorette and birthday party routines at the studio where my company was based. The extra cash infusion helped in a city where a cup of coffee cost a small pile of cash, and gas was more sacred than holy water.

I was feeling slightly nervous, however, since this was the first time teaching in my own studio. If I lost students...well, I couldn't afford to lose students. But I also truly wanted to provide a good experience and show women that they could be sexy and fun and flirty, no matter what age or level of experience.

It didn't take me long to add a few new twists to the lesson plan, and I was feeling significantly fewer butterflies banging around my small intestine by the time my first student moseyed in. Of course it was Barbara Jones, a woman with a nose longer than Pinocchio's, who used it to sniff out gossip like a bloodhound.

"Oh, hello, Misty. It's been so long." Bony Barbara craned her neck around the door. "Am I early?"

"Just on time." I smiled and stood up, waving her into the studio. "How are you?"

"I'm well. Very well." Mrs. Jones vaguely resembled a mouse, and if she had whiskers, they'd be twitching at the moment. I was reminded of my earlier thought that if I could teach Mrs. Jones burlesque, I'd feel just as accomplished as if I'd taught a robot to tango.

She peered at me. "And you? How are you...coping with everything?"

I gave a small, internal sigh while I plastered on a big, fake grin. *Straight to the point*, I thought, though thankfully my mouth said, "Coping with what?"

"Oh, you know." Mrs. Jones glanced around as if looking for a hidden camera. "The whole...Mr. Jenkins business. I heard from Betty Sue, who thought Marianne had heard it at Froggy's."

"Oh, interesting." I looked around. "I'm not sure what they heard, but they wouldn't be letting me teach dance classes if I had been found guilty, now would they?"

I felt like cheese would start oozing from my mouth pretty soon with how fake my smile was—even though Barbara didn't seem to notice. She was too busy making her way over to the closet and poking around places she didn't belong.

"Do you need something?" I asked.

Barbara looked surprised. "I just...I was going to hang my purse up. This isn't a coat closet?"

She flung the door open to the props closet before I had a chance to respond. "Ah...I see. My apologies."

"Those are for class," I said, my voice dripping with sweetness. "Don't worry. By the time you leave, you'll be dressed in nothing but satin gloves and a man's button-down shirt, shimmying your way home."

"Oh, uh. My. That sounds..." Barbara glanced around, but luckily a pretty blonde head bobbed into the doorway at that moment.

"Burlesque?" a high-pitched, girly voice asked. "Am I at the right spot?"

"Yes, absolutely." I tried to mimic the level of sweetness in her voice, but it just didn't come naturally. In fact, it sounded more like a grimace. I cleared my throat and tried again. "Yes...Intro to Burlesque. How are you, Sarah?"

"Oh, wow. That's you!" Sarah pretended to peer closer, her cute blonde hair swinging over her petite shoulders and her clear blue eyes squinting in my direction as if I were a Rorschach blot. "Misty? Wow, you look different."

I resisted the urge to roll my eyes. The email I'd sent had my name on it. There was no surprise I'd be here teaching the class. But I was determined to take the higher road. I could do it. *Take the mature route, Misty.* Plus, the tooth fairy didn't exist anyway. I knew that now. I didn't need to hold a grudge from kindergarten.

I shifted my gaze between Barbara and Sarah. "We're waiting for a few more."

"Who else?" Barbara butted her nose in where it didn't belong once again.

"You'll see," I said. As soon as the words were out of my mouth, the one and only Mrs. Jenkins strolled through the door.

"Well, isn't it just the woman of the hour," Barbara said in a screechy voice. She fidgeted with her hair and tucked her hands first under her arms, then in her pockets, and finally behind her back.

I looked at Mrs. Jenkins to see if she'd say anything about Barbara's insensitive comments. I absolutely didn't want a fight starting here on my first day of classes. This place was starting to feel jinxed.

Sarah yawned fake and loud, and I was grateful for the distraction. "Gosh, I'm tired. Late night yesterday. I'm excited for class though. How many more are coming?"

I was grateful for the distraction, and I spent a few minutes chatting with Sarah over Barbara's pointed questions as the rest of the class trickled into the room.

Despite the fact that I knew most of my students were here solely for morbid curiosity, there was a small twinge of pride in my belly. I'd moved across the country, built up the studio, recovered from the accident that had halted my dancing career.

It'd been one show, one night, and a torn ACL. Months of rehab had left my knee functional again, but I'd never be the same. In addition, the injury had cost me a coveted spot at a well-known dance company along with most of my recurring freelance gigs. Broke, alone, and hurt, I'd finally accepted that it was time to try something new.

I'd been thinking of coming back to Little Lake at some point anyway and wondered if this wasn't a sign the time was right. A few months, some research, and a huge risk later, I'd landed back home.

Looking around at what I had to show for it, a feeling I could only guess was excitement blossomed somewhere in my chest around my heart. I had a gorgeous little studio and a small, but hopefully growing, population of students. Now, if I managed to not get arrested for a crime I didn't commit, that would be a huge bonus.

"We'll start with the basics. First of all, why did you each show up here today?" I stood at the front of my studio and six students spread out before me, some obviously nervous.

The room was silent.

"Oh, come on," I said with a smile. "Something made you click on the Sign Up button. Something dragged you out of the comforts of your homes on this beautiful fall day and back inside a studio. Why?"

Nosy Barbara looked around with shifty eyes. I didn't look in her direction—I knew why she was there.

"Anyone?" I asked cheerfully.

Mrs. Jenkins raised her hand shakily.

"Sure! Mrs. Jenkins. What brought you here today?"

"Well, I'm a widow now. On account of that fact, I gotta get back out there in the dating game sometime in the near future. So I gotta get back into sexy mode." She glanced around. "Y'all ladies know how it is…you get comfortable after a while. I used to be hot, but now I'm older."

The fake smile froze on my face. "Great. Anyone else?" *Please*, I prayed. *Anyone?*

"I'm in a new relationship, actually," Sarah said, swooping in to save the day with another distraction. "I thought it might be a fun way to spice things up. Not that things are *boring* or anything…just…"

"Excellent." I nodded. "Absolutely. It's always fun to add something new *before* things get boring. It can help keep long-term relationships fun and interesting."

Sarah had been my sworn enemy since kindergarten, but at that moment I could've kissed her. After Mrs. Jenkins had spoken, the room went silent. Not a great start to any sort of class, especially one that relied on a loose, fun atmosphere.

"Burlesque is a great way to spice things up at home. In the living room. In the kitchen. Over breakfast. Anywhere." I smiled, more genuinely this time. "The best part, at least for me, is that burlesque is all about feeling comfortable and sexy in your own skin. It's less about the other person and more about becoming a strong, confident woman with a fun spring to your step. If your partner gets enjoyment out of it, that's even better."

With a wink, I dragged a chair to the front of the classroom.

"Let's start slow. We'll do some basic chair work, put you all in some gloves and a feather boa, and then we'll get you all buttoned up in an oversized man's shirt. All things you can find at home or pick up very cheaply."

Walking over toward the radio, I glanced over my shoulder. "Anyone got a song they'd like to start with?" I asked. "Give me something a little sassy."

A few recommendations were shouted out, and I quickly built a playlist in my phone, hooked it up to the stereo, and hit play. As soon as the tunes began pulsing through the speakers, I relaxed. This was my happy place. My comfortable zone. The place where I could go and nobody could disturb me.

"Let's start with a nice little walk. Swing those hips. Good, Barbara!"

I was lying, but Nosy Barbara didn't seem to notice. Instead of swaying her hips, she ticked back and forth like a very robotic clock, but maybe her husband thought her rigid movements were a turn on. Who was I to judge?

"You're a natural." I walked past Sarah and nodded. I was slightly disappointed that my praise wasn't a lie. She moved with a suave grace that only certain people were born with. "Your new boyfriend is a lucky man."

She giggled, and for a moment I thought maybe I could let bygones be bygones. In fact, I was sure of it. Grudges held since kindergarten were a terrible, exhausting way to live. I took a long, deep breath and promised myself I'd try to be better friends with Sarah. After all, maybe it would be fun to get drinks and talk about boys and gossip about bigger cities than Little Lake.

Unlike most people in this town, she had a similar experience as I, in that she left the tiny town and came back. I had visions of us bonding over martinis about traveling, culture, and coming back to the place where we'd started from originally.

"That's it. Maybe a little…less of that." I was afraid Mrs. Jenkins would hip check the girl next to her. Jenkins appeared to be trying out for the National Hockey League as opposed to swaying her hips gently.

"Good, you guys are doing great!" I clicked a button on my phone. "Next song…and we're adding feather boas. Ignore the molting feathers. It might look like a peacock was de-feathered here after class."

I got a small laugh, and the air started to loosen up. Mrs. Jenkins relaxed her hip swaying, the other students stopped looking around at everyone else and began following my lead, and Sarah was truly doing a great job. Even Barbara seemed a bit less robotic, but that could've just been my better mood.

The sixty-minute class flew by, and before I knew it, I was a little sweaty and leading the class in a quick cool down.

"That was really fun," I said, meaning it. "Did you ladies enjoy it?"

"That was great." Sarah gleamed. Not a drop of sweat sparkled on her body, her cute blonde hair looking perfectly smooth. "Really, excellent. Do you have a series coming up?"

I glanced around, pleasantly surprised to find each and every student, with the exception of Barbara, looked back at me expectantly.

"Why…yes! Absolutely." I grinned. "Starts next week—which night works for you all?"

Even Barbara glanced up for a moment before returning her attention back to staring at her big toe.

"Monday. Let's start Monday." Sarah looked at the other ladies, who bobbed their heads in agreement. There were a few "Works for me!"s and a "Kenny can babysit Monday," and we were set.

"It's a date. Thanks everyone for coming. Take your boas with you…and feel free to test them out before class next week."

"What if we don't have anyone to test them out on?" Mrs. Jenkins asked.

An icy silence slithered through the room.

"By yourself, is what I meant," I said, haltingly. "A lot of new dancers don't feel comfortable trying things in front of another person right away. It's always good to try a few songs, find your jam, and practice your favorite mood. That way you're ready whenever the situation arises."

Mrs. Jenkins nodded. "What time Monday?"

"I...uh, how about eight?" I hadn't expected her to be back.

"Works for me. See you girls Monday then." Mrs. Jenkins stood up and began strutting toward the door as if it were a catwalk.

"See you Monday at eight!" I clapped my hands and hoped the students would get to chatting among themselves.

The class had gone so well...and then ended on a sour note with Mrs. Jenkins's awkward question. A smooth closure would have rounded everything out perfectly. Thankfully, Sarah muttered something under her breath that I couldn't hear, and a one or two of the girls laughed. Chatter broke out, and an easy conversation fell into place.

I took the opportunity to gather up a few things, sweep the feathers into the corner, and tidy up the studio to leave it in decent shape before shutting the lights off as the students filed out.

I felt a tap on my shoulder and twirled around to find Sarah standing extremely close to me, hair bobbing with an energy I envied after an hour of dancing.

"Hey, that was a really great class." She reached an arm out and patted me on the shoulder. "Really, I think you're bringing something back to this town that Little Lake desperately needs."

"A beat?" I smiled.

"Some fun! Loosen things up. Everything's so tight-laced around here."

I had a sneaking suspicion that I'd been right—it'd be fun to get to know Sarah. Or to re-get to know Sarah. I certainly wasn't the same person I was in kindergarten, let alone yesterday—why should I expect her to be?

"We should grab a drink sometime," I said. I swung my purse onto my shoulder and shut the lights off in the studio as we stepped out of the room.

"Yeah, definitely. It'd be great to catch up."

I locked the door, glancing at her reflection in the mirror. She looked down the hallway behind her but met my gaze as I turned back.

I nodded. "Absolutely. A lot of time has passed, and we have a lot of chatting to do. I wanna hear all about this *new guy* you have."

"That'll be fun. Say, I've gotta get going…the *new guy* is picking me up downstairs. Let's grab drinks this week."

I began to nod, but Sarah reached out and put a hand on my shoulder.

"If you need anything, though—help, or someone to talk to, or whatever…just let me know."

Generally hating when people, except for Donna, pried into my business, I was surprised to feel a warmness in my stomach. There were tons of stories where old enemies became friends. Maybe Sarah and I would be one of those pairs. After all, they said that love and hate were a very thin line to walk.

"I really appreciate that," I said honestly.

We walked in an easy silence down to the front gates. I slapped my forehead. "Oh shoot, I forgot something in my office. You go ahead. Give me a call this week sometime, and we'll meet up."

"Sure. Time to go test out some of my new moves." Sarah winked.

"You show him, girl." I waved as Sarah took off.

"Hey, actually," I called after her. "Do you have like twenty seconds? I could use your help."

"No problem. What is it?" Sarah looked around the parking lot, probably looking for her ride. But the place was empty, except for a few patrons at Sweets. There was a cop car out front, and I was betting that it belonged to Jax or Alfie. It could be one of the few other cops in town, but since Jax's sister worked at the candy store and Alfie was involved in Jenkins's murder, chances were high it belonged to one or the other. .

"I'm kind of poking around into why someone might have framed me for Anthony Jenkins's death, and I was wondering if you knew any places open late at night around here."

"What kind of places?" Sarah no longer looked around, but focused on me.

"Oh, I don't know...someplace one might go to grab drinks, or...I don't know."

"What makes you think he was out late at night?"

"Someone mentioned that he was out all the time. I figured he was either out at a friend's place, if you know what I mean, or hanging out in some joint, closing the place down."

"I don't know." Sarah sniffed. "I'm not into that sort of thing."

"Of course not," I said quickly. "I just meant if you'd heard something—gossip or whatever. I'm a little bit out of the loop, for obvious reasons."

"I suppose you're right. Who told you that, anyway?"

"I'm not sure I should say..." I glanced around.

"Was she here for class?" Sarah whispered, leaning in.

I gave a quick nod.

Sarah smiled grimly. "Quite the awkward conversationalist."

"Tell me about it."

"Well, actually now that I think about it, I did hear something in the beauty shop just before class."

"Really?" I stepped backward into the building. I wasn't sure this was a conversation I wanted to have in front of a public parking lot where the wife of the victim had been moments before.

"Can I ask what you heard?"

"Did you say you have to run up to your office? What if I walk with you, tell you on the way?"

"Wow, that'd be great. Thank you!"

Sarah lightly grabbed my wrist, and together we walked back up the first flight of stairs. "I was getting my hair done, and of course it was right after Anthony Jenkins's body was found. Naturally, it was the topic of *all* gossip."

"Of course."

"And it did come up that he was always out and about late at night. Now, I'm not sure how accurate this is since it's hearsay, but it might be worth checking out."

"I'm open to anything. I'm at a dead end right now, looking at a long time in prison if this turns out the wrong way."

"Well, apparently he was big into comics. There's this huge underground comic store in the city center. I mean, the place itself isn't huge, but it's not...broadcast at all. The building looks like a dump, there's not a single sign that says comic store, and there's a lot of traffic going in and out of that place that the crowd doesn't want others to know about. I don't know exactly the details, but that's what I've heard. And Anthony's name was attached to it somehow."

"That's could be very helpful, thank you."

"No problem...just don't tell them that you heard it from me."

"Of course not." I'd reached my office and unlocked the door. "Drinks are on me this week."

"Say, let's not get drinks. Let's go to the store together. I'd love to help you with this," Sarah said with wide eyes.

"Really? No, you don't have to do that."

"I want to." She smiled. "I owe you back for that tooth I stole when I was a bratty kindergartener."

"No, don't worry about it. I'd forgotten all about that." *So what?* It was a tiny lie, and I would forget the incident, starting *now.*

"Pretty flowers," she said, glancing over my shoulder.

"Thanks. My friend Donna—you know Donna, who runs Sweets—dropped them off."

Sarah smiled. "Let's head to the store tomorrow together. It'll be fun, an adventure."

"Sure. That sounds great. Do you want me to walk you out? I'm gonna use the bathroom quick and then send out a few quick emails before I lock up." I gestured to the dinky laptop on the desk.

"No problem, I'll let myself out. See you tomorrow!"

* * *

On the way to the bathroom, I found myself humming the tune of a song we'd danced to. A good sign. I washed up and glanced at myself in the mirror, thinking today hadn't gone as poorly as I'd expected. Even my hazel eyes looking back, my still-damp brown hair, my whole perspective looked a bit shinier. With the exception of a few odd lines from Mrs. Jenkins, it'd been a success. And the best part about it was that the girls wanted to come *back*.

Maybe not Nosy Barbara, but I could do without her. I didn't need her money if she only wanted to gather gossip and spit it back out at the salon. I had an official class now. With returning students. Who knew? Maybe business would pick up with a little bit of buzz. They said any publicity was good publicity, so maybe Barbara was doing me a favor after all, spouting about the studio all over town.

I swung by the studio to do a quick check on my way back to the office. All was quiet. The floor still shone bright, but the first scuff marks from the chairs made me feel excited. The stray feathers drifting to the corners were a symbol that the classroom was in use, and the laundry basket full of men's button-down shirts made my heart happy.

I flicked the light switch back off and headed to my office.

There was a slight clink of metal as I approached my office, and I held my breath as a figure stepped out of the office, slowly closing the door behind him.

"Alfie, what are you doing here?" I exhaled my breath in one big swoosh. I took in his stocky figure, made even rounder by a lumpy backpack hanging from his shoulders.

"Misty. Hi, I um...I was just, uh, looking for you."

"Really? What do you need?"

"I wanted to see how things were going. You know, how you're doing...how your first class went," he said stiffly.

"It's fine. But why were you in my office?"

"I just stepped in to wait for you. But when you didn't come back in a minute, I thought I'd come find you up at the studio."

"I'm doing fine, and if you don't need anything from me, I have work to do." I took a step forward, gesturing for him to move out of the doorway.

His short, stubby frame twitched slightly as he glanced around. "Is anyone else here?"

"No. Why?"

He shrugged. "The real reason I'm here is to tell you that we got a phone call from an anonymous source. She said that Mrs. Jenkins was making some trouble in your class."

"Was this female anonymous source a Mrs. Barbara Jones?"

"It's anonymous." A slight line of perspiration broke out along Alfie's hairline. "How did you know it was a female?"

I gave a slight roll of my eyes. I tried to stop it, but it just slipped out. "You said *she*."

"Pretend you didn't hear that." Alfie glanced around. Louder, he said, "It's anonymous."

"Okay, well, on the off chance it was Barbara, I'm guessing she was just trying to stir the gossip pot and give Little Lake something to talk about. For your information, my first class went extraordinarily smoothly, and everyone left happy. Except for Barbara, but I think that's because she can't dance."

Alfie's face reddened to the hue of a licorice rope. I knew it was a low blow, but I didn't appreciate extra drama being generated at my class's expense. There was enough drama and emotion running on overload to fuel a high school cheerleading team.

"I should be going then."

"Yes, I think that's probably best. I have some work to finish up here."

Alfie scooted behind me, lugging what appeared to be a heavy load in that backpack behind him. I wondered why on earth he'd dragged it in here, especially since that was probably his cop car out front, and he could have easily left it in the trunk.

I popped open my laptop and let myself get lost in building a lesson plan for a six-class package. Music streamed from my computer, and it felt satisfying to be in the zone, typing out exercises and moves, "homework" for the students, and a few routines that'd serve as the grand finale for week six. As I typed,

I grew more and more excited for the sessions ahead. Just maybe, it'd work out here in Little Lake. Maybe I'd be able to find my niche.

Thirty minutes later, I stood up and stretched, shutting down my computer and gathering up my things. I glanced around at my little office, happy for a place to call mine. Except there was one thing off—the sunflowers were missing.

"Damn it, Alfie," I growled. He'd toted them off in that backpack, I was sure of it. It wasn't worth the effort of chasing him down to retrieve them, but I'd certainly have a few words ready next time I saw him.

Why on earth would he want my sunflowers? Until now, his unrequited crush was flattering at best, annoying at worst, but this was one step too far. Nobody took my sunflowers.

I shut my lights off and locked the door, thinking maybe it was time to get some cameras installed in this joint. These little surprises were getting old. What I'd give for a nice, normal day.

To cheer me up, I decided to treat myself at Sweets. Some conversation with Donna plus a handful of licorice ropes were exactly what I needed to get my happiness level back up to where it'd been before Alfie'd stolen my flowers.

"Hey, there's the little sexy teacher," Donna called as I walked into the store. A tiny bell jingled, and the warmth of the store combined with the ooey-gooey delicious smell of fudge immediately boosted my happiness level by five points. "How was class?"

"It was great!" I grinned. "Six licorice shoestrings, please. I'm treating myself."

"On the house," Donna said, pulling apart the strands. "We had a few customers stop by after class. It turns out your sessions are good for business. Dancing makes folks hungry. Plus, they all raved about the class. You've got a six-week session coming up next, huh?"

"Yes, things are working out." I sucked on the edge of one licorice rope. "What'd they say, anyway?"

"Oh, you know. Only that you're bringing the hottest thing to come to Little Lake since swing dance."

I allowed myself a huge smile. "It was really a great day. And do you remember Sarah?"

"Sarah...your sworn enemy that moved back here a while ago?"

"Yeah. Well, she's not my sworn enemy anymore. In fact, she's actually supernice, and she signed up for my six-week class. She's a natural."

"That's great." Donna's smile seemed frozen in place. "What's wrong?"

"Nothing," she said, quickly.

I paused. "You're not jealous, are you? I mean, she'll never take your place as my best friend. It's just nice to have one person in class that actually can move to the beat. She's also positive, which helps offset some of the weird stuff Mrs. Jenkins says."

"Oh, of course. And I heard about that. Are you okay?"

"I'm fine. Actually, that didn't bother me as much as Alfie stealing the flowers from my desk after class."

"That turd. Why would he do something like that?"

"Beats me." I leaned on the counter, swallowing the last of my candy. "He's been making little passes at me, so maybe it's some weird thing related to that."

"Sounds like you have a secret admirer." Donna winked.

"No, no...he's just not over our kindergarten fling on the playground." I laughed—Donna knew the story well. "Plus, who 'secretly admires' someone while driving a cop car?"

"He had his cop car here?" Donna peered over my shoulder once more.

"Oh, I thought it was his sitting out front of Sweets. I thought he might've stopped in here, actually. Am I wrong?"

"That's not Alfie's cop car," Donna said, still looking over my shoulder.

"Whose is it then?" I turned to see what on earth Donna was staring at.

"Uh...nothing," she said, all too late.

Because I'd turned around just in time to see Sarah, my sworn enemy, lean up on her tiptoes and kiss my high school sweetheart on the lips.

"Jax," I breathed.

"Hey. *Hey,* earth-to-Misty, are you okay?" Donna asked.

"Yeah, I'm fine." But my voice came out more than a few pitches higher than normal.

"You can talk to me about it."

"What's there to say?" I pried my eyes away from Jax and Sarah. He had one arm wrapped around her waist, a hand situated too close to her rear end for comfort, or at least my comfort, and his lips were completely intertwined with hers. "I'm going to be an adult about this."

Donna's eyes followed me as I reached for more licorice and began taking huge bites of the multicolored rope. Her sympathetic gaze was more than I could handle.

"It's fine. I was just telling you how nice of a person she is. It'd be very immature of me to change my mind only because she's dating my ex."

Donna pursed her lips, watching me shovel more licorice into my piehole.

"Fine," I said, letting my breath whoosh out. "I'm upset. I'm frustrated, but it's stupid, and I realize that."

"It's not stupid. You're allowed to still have feelings for Jax."

"I *don't* have feelings for him. You told me already that he had a girlfriend."

It was catty, but I couldn't help but feel a little betrayed. Donna knew about my rivalry with Sarah, and all she'd said was that Jax's girlfriend was a *b* word. She could've at least given me a heads up.

"I know this looks bad," Donna said, "but I didn't know he was dating Sarah, or else I would have told you. Honestly. Three weeks ago, Jax was dating a different blondie whose chest was larger than Albert Einstein's brains. All of his brains put together."

"That's a lot of brains," I said. I glanced up at her, somewhat relieved for a few reasons. First, because Donna hadn't betrayed me. I mentally kicked myself a bit. Never should I have doubted her friendship. But second, I was relieved because that meant Jax and Sarah were a new, hot item. And statistically, there was a decent chance they'd break up.

I shook my head. "The problem is that she's nice. And she's cute and funny, and there's frankly nothing mean about her anymore. At least not in my class. Dang it!"

"What?" Donna looked alarmed.

"She's a really good dancer too." I threw my hands up. "I can't believe I just gave advice to my archenemy on how to seduce my former boyfriend. That *sucks*."

"It does." Donna placed her hand over mine, which happened to be reaching for the licorice jar once more. "This calls for more. Froot Loops."

I grinned. "You know how to make a girl feel loved."

"I'm *kidding*. Come over and eat dinner today. It's my evening off. Bring your sister—she can play with the kids. It'll be fun."

"Actually, that sounds awesome. I haven't eaten much besides sugar and coffee these past few days. What should I bring?"

"I just told you." Donna winked. "Your sister. And your appetite. I'm having lasagna."

"I'll see you." I tossed a few bucks on the counter and headed out the front door. Jax had swooped Sarah into his cop car, I supposed, when my back had been turned for a few moments.

Better that way, I thought. My stomach couldn't handle seeing any more kisses between the two of them, and I definitely didn't want to come face to face with their relationship. I was fairly certain my vocal chords wouldn't work all that great under those circumstances.

My plans for the rest of the afternoon and evening didn't consist of a whole lot of exciting stuff. I'd finished my emails and class plans at the office, my meals for the week looked like they'd be heated from a can in the microwave, and the television looked as if it'd be my best friend after Donna's house. With nowhere to be, I figured now was a good time to swing by Al's to get my errand out of the way.

Al's was between Sweets and my home, and it was a run-down "convenience" store that sold everything from butter and milk to bullets and hunting knives. I browsed somewhere in between—the BB gun aisle.

"Do you have any pellets, or bullets, or whatever they're called?" I asked Al.

Al's whiskers twitched excitedly. "Which sorta gun? This for your sister? Your brother sent for her gun the other day. Ordered it from here all the way from Montana. I was tickled."

Al didn't understand the internet. He wrote receipts by hand, accepted cash only, and was of the mentality that cell phones and computers were absolutely no-good, useless machines.

"Pellets for whichever gun he got her, then. I'm taking her shooting on Friday."

"You going down to Saddle Ranch?" he asked. Al was short, stout, and blunt. His hair looked as wiry as a scrub-brush's bristles, and the gray strands poking from his ears looked like pipe cleaners. He had more wrinkles than a fat bulldog, and it was clear he'd lived in an era where sunscreen hadn't been a priority.

"This here's your best option," he said, holding out a box. "Thing can go straight through a squirrel if you get 'em at their softest part."

"That sounds...dangerous. Do you have anything less fatal, by chance?"

After a bit of grumbling, he pulled another box off the shelves. "This'll be the weaker stuff you're looking for. Won't kill, only injure."

"Perfect." I took the box and smiled.

"Because we can't trust you with the real stuff, am I right?" Jax's voice sent a chill through my spine.

Al guffawed. "Not after she shot the headlights out of Jerry's truck in high school."

"It was an *accident*," I hissed. "What are you doing here?"

"Swung by to pick up bullets and milk. Where else can I get a combo like that?" Jax winked at Al, who blushed slightly. Jax could even charm the pants off a grizzled, gun-toting, old corner-store owner. No wonder he'd charmed the pants off me. And now, Sarah too.

"Nice of you to pick up your girlfriend from class today," I said, my nose slightly in the air. "I didn't know you knew Sarah."

Jax eyed me warily. Al slowly backed out of the gun aisle and into the lotions area, which was a true sign that he was utterly distracted. Al wasn't the moisturizing type.

"Yeah...well, I met her a few weeks ago at a barbecue, and I'd just broken up with my last girlfriend."

"So she's your rebound. Nice." I rolled my eyes. Why I was acting like a sixteen-year-old with a bad crush was beyond me.

"*No*," Jax said, a bit harshly. "But thanks for teaching her some moves. I'm sure we'll both enjoy them tonight."

"Have a ball." I stalked to the front of the store, where Al was doing his very best to avoid any sort of eye contact with me.

"You have nothing to say about this," Jax called after me. "You've been gone for ten years. And, she's not a suspect for *murder*."

Al gasped as he held the box of BBs. He looked beyond me to Jax. "Can I sell her these?"

"Yeah, yeah. They're not fatal, thank God," Jax said. "But if I show up with a zinger between my eyes, you know who to go after."

"Sure, sure," Al said. "Absolutely, Chief."

* * *

"Is this how things are going to be?" Jax asked, jogging to catch up with me as I headed out of the store.

"Like what?" I kept right on walking.

"This. You. Ignoring me." Jax put a hand on my shoulder and spun me around.

"Would I be talking to you if I was ignoring you?" I asked sweetly.

"You've been gone for ten years. Ten years. What was I supposed to do, wait around?"

I hesitated, glancing around. Jax didn't seem to care that we were in the middle of a parking lot, discussing our personal business for any shopping patrons to hear.

"You're the one who broke off our engagement, Misty. I asked you to marry me. In fact, I *begged* you to stay. You're the one who disappeared, might I remind you?"

I looked into Jax's eyes, unable to decipher the emotion staring back at me.

I cleared my throat and whispered softly, "I'm sorry."

"Sorry for what? You've still never explained why you up and left. But even so, you never came back, didn't look back one damn time at what we had—do you *know* how much that hurt?"

Jax had moved forward, and now his chin hovered just above my lips, which trembled with the close proximity, the emotions between us running deep.

"I *did* come back." My voice shook slightly. "I ran away to college because I didn't know any better. They offered me a full scholarship, and I didn't think I could turn it down."

"Didn't *want* to turn it down..."

"Don't you understand that, Jax?" I peered up at him. "Haven't you ever felt the desire to get up and leave this town, if only for a second? Little Lake will always be here. Don't you understand that urge?"

It was Jax's turn to breathe quietly, at a loss for words.

"Between my crazy family, this nosy town, and my desire to be successful at the one thing I was good at—school— no, it didn't seem like an option to turn down the scholarship."

Jax opened his mouth, then shut it for a moment before he spoke. "But you didn't come back. I didn't hear from you once you left."

Jax had proposed to me the night I graduated high school. He was a few years older, already studying to become a police officer. At the time, I knew we'd had something special, but I figured it would still be there, waiting for me in a few years. Or I'd find someone just as special somewhere else.

Plus, having kids wasn't on the foreseeable horizon for me, and adventure called. I'd been given a full ride to a prestigious college out in Los Angeles—but it came at a cost much larger than tuition. Jax was bound to Minnesota, since he'd already started the police academy. He didn't want to move across the country and start over. His family was here. His life existed in Little Lake.

His proposal had been clear: stay in Minnesota and get married.

There'd been no *long distance* clause or a four-year waiting agreement. It was the ultimate ultimatum. I'd chosen the safer route, or so I'd thought at the time, and I opted for college. Had I been right or wrong? Impossible to say.

"But I did come back," I said softly. "I flew back three weeks later to tell you I was sorry, and I saw you in the window of Lenny's with another girl. You'd moved on."

I cleared my throat, beads of dampness lining the corners of my eyes. I couldn't look at Jax, but I could feel his gaze on me. Without a word, he strode past me and climbed into his cop car without looking back. Just as I'd done ten years before, driving off to California.

A small sniff escaped, but I refused to cry anymore over my past. As they said, *every sinner has a future, and every saint has a past.* My past just happened to be not all sunshine and roses and smart decisions. Because as it turned out, college wasn't my calling after all. But burlesque had been just around the corner.

I'd dyed my hair neon pink and purple ombré, slipped into my first pair of fishnets, and the rest was history. I'd vowed never to let school keep me from following my heart ever again.

CHAPTER TEN

———

As luck would have it, I ran into one of my new dance students as she pulled up and parked.

"Hey, Misty," Anna said. She had longish brown hair, a quiet disposition, and a sweet smile.

"Hey! How are you, Anna? I'm just headed home. Taking my sister shooting on Friday." I held up the pack of BBs sheepishly.

"Oh, that's great. I wouldn't trust myself around a squirt gun, let alone a BB gun." She winked. "But I imagine it's great bonding time."

"Oh, of course." A sudden thought occurred to me. "Actually, do you have a cell phone I could use really quick? I was going to stop over to her place, but I don't have my phone with me."

"Ah...I hate when I forget mine."

She pulled a demure, dark-brown case out of her purse and handed it over. "There's no pass code."

"Thanks." I smiled and turned away. She didn't need to know that *not having my phone with me* was code for *didn't need it, since it didn't have service anyway.*

"What's up, Sis?" I listened for a moment as Harmony excitedly greeted me. "Hey listen, I'm coming to get you. Feel like playing with Donna's kids tonight?"

"Yay!" Harmony shrieked. "I'll get all my stuff ready."

"It's just dinner. No need to pack a suitcase."

"But I need books, and I got a new craft weaver that I want to show Lisa, and I also—"

"Yeah, yeah. As long as it can fit in a backpack and you don't whine when it's time to go. I'll be there soon."

I hung up. "Thanks a lot, Anna."

"You're good friends with Donna?"

"Yeah, we've been best buds for a long time," I said.

"Ah...so you must know her brother, then?"

"Her brother?"

"Jax," she said.

"Oh...yeah. Vaguely." Even though his name warmed me to the depths of my soul. Whether out of anger or passion or love or confusion, I couldn't be sure.

"Man, he's *scorching*." Anna fanned herself. "I didn't know he was going out with Sarah from class. I'm envious. A cop *and* a hunk...all from small town Little Lake, born and raised? Whooooeee."

"Yeah, I think they're a new couple."

"That's why I hadn't heard anything. Ah, well. Maybe they'll break up, and we'll all get our chances—am I right?" she tittered.

I gave her a halfhearted smile that I hoped passed for whole-hearted. "I gotta get going. Sister's waiting."

"Of course. See you Monday!"

With a quick wave, she was off into Al's. It was still only late afternoon, so I had some time to kill before heading over to Mom's to pick up Harmony. Walking the short distance home, I ran through my mental checklist of things to knock out with my extra time. Maybe a shower wouldn't be so bad. I took a whiff of myself. Definitely, a shower couldn't hurt.

I headed up my driveway a few minutes later, lugging the BBs under my arm. I pressed the kitchen door open, deposited the BBs on the sink, and took a quick handful of Froot Loops from my backup stash above the sink. I needed energy somehow to power through a shower and make it to Donna's, and then proceed to have enough energy to deal with her cute, energetic little rug rats. All five of them.

I jogged up the steps, skipping the crooked one, and headed into my bathroom. Climbing into the shower, I cranked the water as hot as I could handle and let it wash over me.

When I heard the first thunk, I thought I'd bumped my elbow against the wall. But when the second thump sounded even louder than the first, I shut off the water. The sound of footsteps sprinting down my stairs—the stairs *inside my house*—was unmistakable.

Someone had broken in while I'd been showering.

Or—a thought sent chills up my spine—someone had been inside this whole time, and I'd happened to catch them in the middle of their snooping.

I froze, my heart leaping into my throat and pulsing in my ears. The silence was so absolute that my thoughts sounded loud. The front door, or so I guessed from upstairs, banged as if it'd been flung open against the wall.

Grabbing the fluffy blue towel from the rack next to the shower, I leapt onto the mat, enveloped myself in the cloth, and hightailed it to the stairs. *I should probably call the police* was a passing thought that came into my head and then flew right on out of it.

There'd be time to call the police after I caught a glimpse of the intruder. Chances were high it was related to Anthony Jenkins's murder. If that was the case, I needed to find the intruder. This terrorizing, first of my studio and now of my home, needed to stop.

By the time I skidded into the entryway, the flapping front door hung slightly crooked on its hinges, and a huge black mark was gouged out of my wall where the knob had cracked into the paint. I flew out the door, still dripping wet and clothed only by the towel.

"Stop," I shouted, running a few paces down the driveway.

A figure bolted away down the road, a bulky, dark-gray sweatshirt and black sweatpants disguising the basic outline of the person. The person was fast. The figure leapt onto a bicycle that'd been stashed off to the side of the road a few blocks down. I hadn't noticed it during my lackadaisical trip home, as it'd been tossed into some lilac bushes.

My shoulders heaving, breath coming in huge gulps, I slowed my pace. I came to a complete stop a few steps later, and put my hands on my knees. I'd never be able to capture the intruder while I was barefoot and they were shoed. Especially if they had a bike. Or a...*a cop car?*

The intruder stopped a few blocks down the road, and if I hadn't raced out into my driveway, I never would've noticed the fact that there'd been a cop car parked at the gas station. The man, or so I assumed, threw his bike into the trunk of the cop car, hopped in the front seat, and squealed away, lights blinking blue and red.

There's no way I would've been able to catch a bicyclist. But there was *definitely* no way I'd be able to catch a car. Especially one with flashing lights.

Eventually, I picked up my spirits enough to reenter my home. This time, I took careful stock of where everything was placed as I slowly swept my way through my grandmother's old house. Nothing in the kitchen seemed amiss, or in the living room, dining room, or the den. In fact, the first floor seemed completely untouched, except for my now-slightly-crooked door and the black ding mark against the wall.

Before I went upstairs, I considered calling the police. But I realized that calling the cops on themselves wasn't the best plan I'd ever had. Not to mention, I couldn't even act on the plan if I wanted.

Get a phone, Misty, I told myself. *So you have the option to call someone.*

First thing tomorrow, I'd stop at Al's. Even if I only had ten dollars to my name, I was getting a ten-dollar phone. Or a walkie-talkie, whichever worked better.

Oh well, it was time for me to head to Donna's house anyway. I considered rescheduling but decided against it for multiple reasons. The first was easy, as I didn't have a phone to reschedule *with*. Also, I didn't exactly feel like being alone tonight. It was a bit creepy being in this old home all by myself, knowing that someone else had been in here with me while I was showering minutes before.

I trooped upstairs, anxious to discover the damage that'd been done. It was looking less and less like it had been a random burglary, based on the fact that none of my things were taken.

A simple thief would've at least grabbed *something*. Although, in his defense, it's not like I had a lot of stuff lying around to grab, anyway. When I reached my bedroom, nothing immediately looked astray. My purse, credit card, and the single pair of tiny diamond studs my grandmother had given me were all safe and sound, just where I'd left them. More and more, I felt confused. What did the culprit want?

If he'd been there to hurt me, then why had he run away?

If he'd been here to take something, had I scared him away, or did I simply not have what he was looking for?

Seeing nothing out of place in any of the rooms I checked, I returned to my bedroom and grabbed a sweatshirt and my stretchiest pair of jeans. One needed to be able to binge after a nerve-wracking event like this one.

Reaching for my sock drawer, the realization that something was off hit me. My fishnet stocking drawer was slightly ajar. I'd closed it this morning for sure. It bothered me when drawers were open a titch, so almost a hundred percent of the time, I kept my drawers shut firmly.

"So strange," I muttered. "Fishnets?"

I yanked the drawer the rest of the way open. It was impossible to tell whether or not anything was missing, since I had a plethora of stockings, none of them matched up in pairs. I wasn't a huge fan of wasting time rolling my socks together.

I poked around a bit more. Maybe they were looking for money, I thought. That gave me a chuckle. If they wanted money, all they needed to do was show up at my studio—that's where all my money had gone. Into the sparkly mirrors, the shiny floors, and the men's shirts dangling from the closet. Any money I hadn't spent there had gone to the measly stocked pantry full of dry pasta noodles and boxes of Froot Loops.

I stretched up, scanning the rest of my room and not seeing anything else terribly out of place. I was starting to feel a bit of the heebie-jeebies being in my home alone, especially with no phone, so I quickly threw on some comfy yoga pants instead of the jeans, and a droopy, white knit sweater. A quick glance in the mirror above my dresser, and I deduced I was ready to rock and roll, the off-the-shoulder sweater even making me feel a bit fancy.

I gave the fishnet-stockings drawer a once-over again, but if anything was missing. it was one measly stocking. There was nothing else to take.

The next thought struck me like a gong: What if it was the killer, coming by to take more of my stockings for another murder?

My heart rate sped up exponentially, and the creepy-crawly feeling intensified, the tiny hairs at the nape of my neck prickling. With no car and no phone, now was not the time to be a half mile away from my neighbors. I slung my purse over my shoulder and hustled out the front door. Though I locked it and double-checked it twice, it didn't make me feel much safer. Plus, the sun was sinking, and by now it was almost dinnertime.

I scurried down the road in the direction of my mother's house, glancing over my shoulder the entire while. I couldn't shake the feeling that a missing stocking was a bad sign, both for me and for the next victim.

CHAPTER ELEVEN

———

"Lasagna is served. Feet off the table, Alec." Donna's singsong voice drew everyone's attention, and six little pairs of legs rushed toward the heaping pile of meat, sauce, and noodles that smelled *out of this world*.

"Nathan's working tonight?" I ruffled Harmony's hair and gave her a gentle push in the direction of Donna's stampede of kids. It didn't take much convincing, and soon she was shrieking with the rest of them over who could blow their homemade straw wrappers the furthest.

"Yeah, he'll be back sometime around two a.m.—I think." Donna scooped huge slices onto everyone's plate, ending with her own. "Sit down, eat. You're withering away."

"The sugar and espresso diet," I muttered quietly enough so that the kids couldn't hear. "I should write a book about it."

Donna was already chewing her food, slapping a kid's wrist, and catching a water glass from tipping over. I'd never felt like more of an underachiever in my life. All I was doing was eating and talking, which I considered a pretty good feat as long as food wasn't falling from my mouth.

"Eat up," Donna said, tilting her head in my direction.

And she could carry on a conversation? This woman was a superhero.

I'd walked in with Harmony in hand minutes before, the break-in to my home fresh on my brain. I wanted to vent to Donna, get a little angry, maybe a little scared, and then have her calm my frazzled nerves. All thoughts had flown out of my head in the minutes since arrival. The chaos here was enough to make anyone's thoughts disappear.

A small part of me felt a bit sad that Donna now had kids of her own. I'd always been the one she soothed, the one whose hair she held as I puked, and the one who she told to stop studying and get to bed. Now, she had her own family to attend to, and I had...well, I had myself. Growing up was tough.

"What's on your mind, chickie?" Donna asked. Through the hustle and bustle that was her dining room, she still managed to sense when I was off.

My eyes smarted as I set my fork down. *Dang emotions!* They were cropping up everywhere now that I was back. When I'd been in LA, I'd cried once during my ten years there, and only then...due to the ACL incident that'd put an end to my dancing career.

"Spill it." Donna leaned over and lightly whacked my hand with her spoon. "And I don't mean those tears. Spill the beans."

"Someone broke into my grandmother's house." I scooted my chair closer and spoke in low tones.

Donna's eyes widened. "First of all, it's *your* house. Get used to it, because I'm not letting you sneak away again. Second of all, what the *what*? Did you call the cops?"

I opened my mouth to speak, but Donna bulldozed right ahead. "What did they take? How do you know? Are you *okay*?"

One of Donna's kids—Alec, or one who looked just like Alec—stared up at me with wide eyes. Maybe he could tell I was upsetting his mother.

"Eat up, Drew," Donna said. "Dinner's gonna get cold, and Alec just stole your bun."

Squeals and a small scrabble broke out over the pilfered bun, and Donna turned back to me. "So? Are you all right?"

"I'm fine. They must have hid when I walked in. Then I took a shower, and that's when they escaped. They ran through my front door, and from what I can tell, they didn't take anything of importance."

"Did they take anything at all?"

I shrugged.

"What does that mean?"

"It means..." I glanced at the table. Harmony looked up at me for a second but dived right back into her lasagna with a huge grin on her face. "I have a bad feeling that it was the same person that killed Anthony Jenkins. My stocking drawer was open, and I have a million pairs of fishnets in there not bundled up. It's impossible to tell if anything is missing, but the drawer was ajar, and I'm sure I shut it."

"You do always keep your drawers shut...drove me nuts in high school." Donna chewed thoughtfully. "But how do you know it wasn't random? Maybe it was just someone looking for some extra dough lying around, and they thought to check your sock drawer. Maybe they just didn't expect...sexy socks."

"I considered that. But, it doesn't feel random." I shook my head. "Maybe I'm being paranoid, but this whole Anthony thing hasn't been resolved yet, so I'm still not off the hook."

"And you can't afford to *not* be paranoid."

"Exactly. I feel like they were looking for something. What exactly, I don't know. But my gut tells me it's not random."

"That's a lie. You don't have a gut—you've been getting skinnier. Eat up."

"I didn't—"

"You didn't call the police," Donna finished. "I assumed, what with no phone and no car. It's no matter. Jax will be here in a few minutes. He's swinging by after his shift."

My eyes went big. "Did you tell him I'd be here?"

"No." Donna looked down at her plate. "He's over all the time. He lives next door and doesn't have a wife to cook, so he stops by often."

"You're lying. Donna, you knew it would be awkward between us."

"Why should it be awkward between you? Alec—eat it. If you butter that bun one more time, you yourself will turn into a stick of butter, and you won't be able to go to your swimming lessons tomorrow because you'll be too slimy."

Alec giggled, and Donna turned her gaze back to me. "Why, Misty? It's been *ten years*. I love you. I love my brother. Is it too much to ask that you can be in the same room at the same time?"

"No." I paused, hanging my head a bit. "It's just..."

"What did you do?"

"I had a run-in with him at Al's after the whole thing at Sweets earlier today. I was kind of a snot about him dating Sarah."

Donna raised one eyebrow, a smile quirking at the corner of her mouth. "Really."

"Shut it."

"You still have feelings for him."

"Do not."

"Do too. What did Sarah ever do to you?"

"She stole my tooth!"

"As an adult, Misty. What did Sarah do to you except go out with Jax? You were just talking about how much you liked her."

I let out a long exhale. I knew what the right answer was, but I wanted to pretend the answer was something entirely different. "Fine. I'll apologize."

"I didn't say that." Donna flicked her gaze sideways. "I don't care if you pour your pretty little broken heart out to him, so long as I can have dinner with my best friend and my brother in the same night. At the same time. At the same place."

"My heart is not *broken*—"

"Look who's here! Uncle Jax." Donna could've winked at me, or maybe she blinked or twitched or anything else unintentional, but I didn't buy it. She had ulterior motives, and I just had to figure out exactly what they were.

Donna stood, wiping her hands on her trendy jeans as she walked toward the front door amid the herd of children trying to break it down.

"She's very stylish," Harmony pointed out, still sitting at the dinner table next to me. She eyed my clothes judgmentally.

"Yeah, yeah..." I eyed Donna once more. I hadn't envied my friend, only wished the best for her. Our life goals, visions, and dreams had been so entirely different from one another's that there was virtually no competition between us. I wanted to be wild and free. She wanted to have a large family and stay in a small town. It was part of the reason we made such a good pair.

But now as I looked at her busy life, a part of me was jealous of how content she seemed. Of course I was happy for my friend, but part of me wanted to figure out how to discover what I wanted. What my life was missing. Donna filled the role of mother and wife and store owner so easily, it was as if she was made for the job. But me, I had a struggling dance studio and practically a warrant out for my arrest.

"It's okay." Harmony reached over and squeezed my hand. "I love you even if you decide to never wear jeans again."

I had a retort at the ready, but it slid from my lips as Donna flung the door open and Jax stepped into the warm, crazy household. He didn't notice me, occupied with the kids climbing up his legs and hanging from his taut arms.

I savored the moment of anonymous creeping before he realized I was watching him. He was a natural with the kids. Tickling one, fluffing another's hair...when Alec kicked him in the shin, Jax picked up the kid by both arms and looked him in the eye. "I'm bigger than you, buddy, so don't you go kicking me, or I might just have to sit on you."

A giggle slipped from my lips as Alec nodded very seriously, his eyes bugging out of his head. It was obvious Jax was the main attraction in this household.

I took another bite of pasta, trying to ignore the painful tugs on my heart. Had I really left all of this in search of something better?

Jax's eyes slid over to meet mine, and I gave a half smile while trying to chew, which didn't work out particularly well. On the contrary, I lost a noodle down the wrong pipe and ended up hacking half a lung into my water glass, or just about.

"Someone's excited to see me," Jax said. He gave Donna a stern look. "What are you doing here, Misty?"

I pounded myself on the chest, *not* a sexy way of greeting someone. When I inhaled enough air to breathe, I choked out my answer. "I"...*cough*..."I was invited"...*dying*..."invited for dinner."

"Strange. As was I." He turned toward Donna. "In fact, my sister *insisted* I be here tonight. She even made my favorite dish for the occasion..."

Both of us looked at Donna. Jax's arms were crossed, and I had a hand on my hip.

"Let's eat!" she said faux cheerfully. "Jax, you can have my seat next to Misty. I am all done eating, and in fact, I gotta go get the twins ready for bed. Alec, Drew—come on."

I didn't think steam was coming out of Jax's nose, but it might've been close. There was a ninety percent chance he was only upset that Donna had conned him into coming over. The other ten percent could've been that he was plain old mad at me.

"We'll eat. Right after I have a word with your brother." I smiled at Donna, slipped one hand on Jax's wrist, and pulled him into a tiny closet off to the side of the hallway. When I initially opened the door, I hoped it would be a study or a lounge or the den, but I was out of luck. It was her vacuum closet. Luckily, there was a single light bulb above us that had a thread dangling from it.

I reached up between our noses and gave a single yank. The light flicked on, and Jax and I were face to face, chest to chest, toe to toe in the cramped space.

"Seven minutes in heaven?" Jax crooked an eyebrow. "That's all I got."

"Good thing it won't take you that long," I shot back, knowing it was a lie. "I'm sorry." I kept my fists balled at my sides. I didn't know whether to touch him, look away, or meet his gaze. "I'm sorry I acted like an immature brat at the store today."

"Why?"

"Why am I sorry?" I paused. "Because I shouldn't be acting like a tween."

"Why do you care who I date?"

"Sarah was my archenemy from kindergarten." I brushed a strand of hair away from my lips, where it'd stuck. I couldn't get the hair to move, so I ignored it. "It wasn't about you. It was about her."

"Really." Jax reached up and moved the hair, taking his long, slow time. "Kindergarten grudges. That's something else."

"Do you hold grudges?" I asked, my eyes peering into his, trying to read his expression.

"Depends."

"Hmm."

"Not usually."

I smiled. "Can we be friends for Donna's sake?"

"I didn't say that I let my grudges against you go."

"Hrmph. I'm trying to be an adult here. You're not helping."

"Did you really come back to visit?"

I nodded, staring at my toes. I suddenly wished the light bulb would flick off of its own accord, shedding us in darkness. There was something about the cover of blackness that made difficult subject matters easier to talk about.

"Then I have no grudge against you." Jax tipped my chin upward and looked into my eyes. "But if I find out you have anything to do with this Jenkins business…"

I shook my head *no*, but I knew what I was about to say would contradict that entirely. "Speaking of…"

Jax groaned. "What now?"

"I caught someone breaking into my house today."

"Did you file a report?"

"Yes."

"Good. What did the cop on the clock have to say? It's weird I didn't hear a call come in."

"It's not *actually* that weird…not since I didn't actually call it in," I said, wincing.

"Didn't you say you filed a report?"

"Yeah…well, I guess technically I'm filing one right now."

Jax's eye roll was impressive.

"What? You're the chief."

"I thought you didn't know I'd be here."

"I didn't. I was going to call, then Donna…never mind." With a shudder, I continued. "I think it was the killer."

"Are you okay?" Jax put his hands on each of my biceps, analyzing me with the sterile intent of a doctor. The remnants of passion and emotion were gone, filled with mild concern for my safety.

"I'm fine." I wanted to push him away, but his touch felt so good I didn't move. "But the other reason I couldn't call it in…was because the culprit drove away in a cop car."

"What?"

"I chased the guy out of my house. Then he got on a bike and pedaled to the gas station, where he got in the cruiser and drove away with the lights on."

"Did you see who it was?"

"No. A guy in a gray sweatshirt and sweatpants. Oh God..." A thought crossed my mind. "What if it was Alfie digging through my underwear?"

"It wasn't Alfie."

"How do you know?"

Jax paused. A thought flitted across his eyes, I could tell. But I couldn't read what it was.

"Was he working today?" I asked.

"Yes, but I'll have to look at the time cards...he didn't respond to a stolen bicycle call this afternoon." Jax bit his lip, as if realizing he shouldn't be telling me this. "Why do you think he was digging in your underwear drawer, anyway?"

"Well..." I squirmed. "He's kind of been coming on to me lately, and the only thing I noticed that was off in my house was the drawer where I keep my fishnet stockings."

An almost-amused gleam took residence in Jax's eye. "Huh."

"Don't judge."

"I'm not."

We were at a standstill for the moment.

"Nothing else is missing?" Jax asked.

"No, not that I know of. I pretty much locked up and headed over here."

"I'm going to call some men I trust, send them over with Nathan as a watchdog, just to make sure there's no funny business if it is a cop. I'll have them look at your place. Do you have keys on you?"

I nodded.

"Give them to me. I'll have Nathan swing by on the way."

"Does Nathan usually help out with police work?" I asked.

"Nathan is helping out because I trust him," Jax said. "And also because people he loves are involved, so if I don't include him, he'd never leave me alone."

"Brothers-in-law," I said with a smile.

Jax didn't return my grin. "We'll figure this out. I promise."

My smile faltered. I sure hoped so. I had a lot of things to figure out, including the man standing before me. "Are we okay here?" I asked. "At least for now?"

Jax nodded. "I'm sorry to hear your house was broken into. If you really do need anything, please let me know. And I don't know what this business with the cop car was, but until we figure it out, I want you coming straight to me. Do you understand?"

I nodded.

"We've had our...ups and downs, but I don't want anything to happen to you." Jax lightly cupped my chin, and for a moment I was transported back into high school, when he would stare into my eyes as we cuddled with piles of blankets in the back of his beat-up Ford truck at the drive-in.

"I know," I whispered.

"I'll never stop caring about you. We didn't work out, that's all. Timing is a big part in any relationship. It does no good putting the blame on either of us."

The dull flame that'd been burning in my stomach ever since I'd come back to Little Lake and seen Jax sparked to something more. "You're a good man."

Jax looked up, away from my line of sight.

I took the opportunity to examine his face, which had only become more handsome and rugged with age. His eyes hosted more sadness than the carefreeness they'd carried in high school, and the mischievous gleam had morphed into a devilish determination. Probably due to years of experience on the job.

I cleared my throat. "Is ten years long enough to put our differences behind us and be friends?"

Jax gave a small smile, one that didn't quite crease the endearing laugh lines around his face, and gave a quick nod.

"Plus, I really like your girlfriend. I was just being a brat earlier at the store. She's different than I remembered her." I laughed. "Hell, she can even *dance*. She seems very sweet, and she helped make my class flow a lot smoother today. In fact, she even volunteered to help me figure out this whole Anthony Jenkins mess. We're going to some comic store together."

Jax's forehead creased. "When are you going?"

"Don't worry. I'm not dragging her into anything unsafe. She overheard some gossip that Anthony frequented this place late at night, so we're going to go check it out. If there's anything dangerous, I won't bring her into it. I promise."

"If there's anything dangerous, I don't want *you* going into it."

I raised an eyebrow. "Well, I don't have much of a choice if I want to find the person who was in *my* studio, in *my* house, and killing *my* landlord. I didn't do it, Jax."

"I'll help you out where I can," Jax said. "When are you going? I'll go with."

"You can't go with. Everyone knows you're a policeman, and they won't talk as freely as they would with two—"

"With two beautiful young women," he interrupted

I gave a hesitant smile. "I was going to say with two chicks who don't work for the law."

Jax let out a guffaw. "Then you don't know the comic store type. They're more scared of girls than they are cops."

I grimaced. "True. But it's worth a shot. I promise I'll call you if anything appears at all fishy."

"When are you going? I'll make sure I'm in the area. I'll throw your BB gun in my trunk, just in case."

I made a face. "Tomorrow night."

Jax paused. "Really?"

"Yeah, why?"

"I assume you're going to the sketchy comic store down in the city center."

"Yeah."

"They're not open tomorrow night."

"Are you sure?"

"I'm positive." Jax bit his lip. "One or two of the cops hang out there. They always request to work on the nights that the joint isn't open. They're dedicated frequenters of the place, let me tell you—spend all their free time there. If they had the night off and the place wasn't open, they'd have no idea what to do with themselves."

"Hmmm. Okay, well. I'm sure Sarah didn't know. She's probably never been there before. I'll give her a call and see if she wants to reschedule."

"We should head back out to dinner. We'll only give Donna a little crap for being so sneaky, playing this setup game to get us both here at one time."

"Sounds good." I smiled. "Pinky swear we can be friends? For old time's sake?"

Jax's brown eyes melted into gooey chocolate, and his grin took on a painfully charming quirk. "I like our pinky swears."

I blushed. It'd been our *thing* in high school. We'd pinky sworn never to leave each other. That'd been the day before he'd proposed and I'd run for the hills. I'd never expected a proposal so soon.

"This time, I mean it." I smiled and held my hand out.

Jax encircled my pinky with his, and we both kissed our respective thumbs. His lips grazed his thumb for a longer time than necessary, and a flutter took off in my stomach.

He shook me out of my wandering thoughts with a firm shake of our pinky fingers.

I glanced back up at him. "One more thing. Could I borrow your cell phone?"

"Where's yours?"

"It's at home." Technically this was true. I just didn't add that it also didn't have a plan or minutes attached to it and was about as useful as a dead log.

"Why didn't you bring it with? Your home gets broken into, and you walk over here all alone with no phone?"

I crossed my arms. "Yup."

"The thing doesn't work, does it?"

"Nope."

Jax sighed. "Here. If you don't have a phone by tomorrow, I'm assigning you an old one from the station."

"I'll get one."

"Fine." Jax handed it over. "Who are you calling?"

"Your girlfriend. I gotta let her know that the shop is closed tomorrow."

Jax unlocked his phone and handed it over. "I could just tell her, you know."

"I'd rather do it. Maybe she'll want to reschedule." I scrolled through his contacts. "Do you have her number in here?"

"Oh. Yeah." His cheeks tinged pink. "Let me find it."

"Uh, uh, uh!" I dangled the phone behind my back. "What did you name her? We're friends. We can talk about these things."

"*I* didn't name her."

"Then who did?" I winked.

"She entered it on our first date."

"Oh, for cute. And what did she enter it under?"

Jax cleared his throat. "Let me—"

"No, let *me*." I gave him a light punch on the arm. "Be a pal."

Jax looked me in the eye, trying to maintain some dignity. "Schnookie."

"Mmm. For *real* cute."

"Shut up." Jax turned and stalked out of the closet, yanking the chain on the light and slamming the door behind him.

In darkness, I hit the dial button on the screen. "Talk to me, Schnookie."

The phone rang, and an innocent, childlike voice answered. "Sugar Pie, how you doing?"

"Hi, uh. This is actually Misty Newman. I...uh, where to start. It's a bit of a long story."

"Okay..." Rightfully so, Sarah sounded a bit skeptical as to why I was using her boyfriend's phone. Little did she know, I'd also dragged him into a closet, and though my intentions had been (mostly) innocent, it didn't sound all that great when I said it aloud.

"My house was broken into tonight, and I didn't have a phone to call the police from. So I ran over to my friend Donna's house, well, you probably know Donna—Jax's sister—to use hers. Jax happened to be here, so I just reported the crime to him instead of using her phone."

"I'm still not sure why you called me..."

"Oh, right." I did an eye roll at myself. "I'm sorry. The point I was *getting* to was that I mentioned to Jax you and I were going to hang out and visit the comic store tomorrow, and he said it was closed. I just wanted to let you know so we didn't make the trip down there for nothing. Maybe we can reschedule?"

"Why did you tell Jax?"

"I don't know. I just mentioned it offhand."

"Ah. What did he say?"

"Not much. He told me not to get you in trouble."

Her laugh tinkled on the other end of the phone. "I do that enough myself, I guess."

"I don't think that's what he meant." I clicked the light back on, realizing I'd been standing in the dark. "I think he meant I'm a bad influence on you, and he'd like to keep you around, all in one piece."

"Sorry to hear about your break-in. Are you okay?"

"I'm fine. Thanks for asking. I scared them away."

"Who was it?" she asked. "Do you know?"

"I'm not sure who it was...I only caught a glimpse of their back as they ran away. They wore baggy clothes."

"Ah, well, I'm glad you're okay."

"Thanks, I appreciate that. But enough bad news. Did you want to reschedule our visit to the comic store?"

"I'm not sure," Sarah said. "It might not be such a good idea. I mean no offense, but if people are breaking into your house and stuff, maybe I shouldn't be publicly asking about it around town."

I bit my lip. "Of course not. Absolutely, that's a much smarter thing to do. I shouldn't have even asked."

"It's not that—I'd still love to help in any way I can, maybe just not so much in the public eye. In fact, if you want to bounce ideas off of me or vent or anything like that, I'm always here."

"Great. Thanks."

There was a small pause as I waited to see if she had anything else to say.

"Call me if you need anything," she added.

"Will do. See you in class Monday, if not before."

Sarah clicked off the line.

Now that Sarah was out, I needed a backup plan. Stat. I was sick of hiding out in my home, walking on eggshells, and sneaking into closets. Well, not so much the latter, but that was only because it was hardly punishment being pushed nose to nose with Jax.

I rejoined the party that hadn't stopped with my absence in the dining room. The kids now had ice cream face paint on their lips and cheeks, and the smell of strawberry, chocolate, and vanilla hung potent in the air.

One glance at Harmony was enough to tell me she'd had enough sugar to sustain her energy levels for the next three hours. The crash that followed would be quick and hard, I was certain. Donna and Jax sat at the dining room table, talking in low voices. Each had a glass of wine, Donna's significantly emptier than Jax's, who was busy shoveling in bites of lasagna between phrases.

They both looked up as I entered the room, their mouths halting movement at exactly the same time. They looked more like twins at this moment than siblings, Jax the older brother and Donna the youngest.

"Don't stop on my account." I sat down at the empty seat on the other side of Jax. I lazily draped my arm over his shoulder. "PS, we're friends now."

"I see that." Donna took a sip of wine, and her cheeks brightened. "Good to see."

"What'd she say?" Jax asked as I handed him his phone back.

"Schnookie said she doesn't want to reschedule." I smiled at Donna. "Schnookie, can you believe it? What's it been, like three weeks?"

"I don't call her that," Jax growled.

"Okay then, Sugar Pie," I said.

He looked away.

"Fill me in," Donna said. She reached over and poured me a glass of wine.

I took a few sips before I began. I recounted the afternoon's events to Donna, hitting the high points like making plans with Sarah, chasing away an intruder, and finding out that the store would be closed tomorrow.

"I don't want to wait," I groaned. "I don't have *time* to wait for the place to open."

"Let's go tonight." Donna finished her wine, then reached over and started on Jax's still-full glass.

"No," Jax said, just as I said, "Sure!"

"No," Jax said again. "Who would watch the kids?"

"You?" I asked, at the same time Donna said firmly, "You."

Jax stood, a bit wobbly as he tried to scoop one more bite of lasagna into his mouth and push his chair back. "No, thank you. No can do. I like kids, but this many is…impossible."

"Crack open a beer, turn the television on, and watch football. Make sure none of the kids kill each other, listen for sounds of screaming, and don't let Alec eat his chalk. It *doesn't* taste like strawberry, and it's *definitely* not edible."

"Have you tried it?" I asked.

Donna raised an eyebrow but didn't stop talking. "Please? You don't want Misty to go alone."

"And you can't go poking around, since you're a cop, and we've talked about that," I said.

"Fine." Jax sat down heavily.

"We'll be quick. I promise." Donna plowed ahead. "Nathan is close by, anyway. You just told me he's headed to Misty's house to look around. I'll tell him to swing by here to help until we get back."

"Where's your beer?" Jax finished his food and started for the kitchen with his dirty dish in hand.

"Right hand side of the fridge—and thanks! You're the best." Donna leapt up and grabbed my wrist. "Adventure!"

I smiled, hoping for more than an adventure.

I wanted answers.

CHAPTER TWELVE

_____

After Donna's speech to the kids, which included things like no sword fights, no nudity, and mandatory toilet flushing, we encountered a last warning from Jax, who was already looking like he needed earplugs and serious Advil.

I kissed Harmony on the head and promised I'd be back soon, but she was already tugging Jax's finger and begging for an action movie instead of a princess one. My little feminist. Donna and I slipped out after another ten minutes of good-byes and hugs from little hands. When we reached her car, the silence felt almost cold.

"Pretty crazy, huh?" Donna asked as we got inside. "I bet that doesn't make you want kids."

"A little," I said, honestly. But another small part of me disagreed.

"But?"

I smiled. My best friend could always read my mind. "There's something nice about having a bunch of people who love and care about you, running around all loud and chaotic. It keeps life interesting, or so it seems."

"Interesting, yes. Stressful, yes. Glamorous, no."

"But you love it?"

"I wouldn't trade it for the world." Donna reached a hand over. "You'll find it someday too, if and when you want. And if and when you do, you'll know."

We rode to the city center in silence. I couldn't tell what Donna was thinking about, but I had a lot running through my mind. Everything from kids and families, intruders stealing fishnet stockings, and comic books, of which I knew nothing. The latter scared me the most.

It was a good thing the drive took only five minutes. Otherwise, I would have probably talked myself out of going before we pulled into the dark, gray alley Donna's phone GPS directed us to.

"This can't be right," she muttered. "I've lived here for *how* many years, and I never knew this was here?"

"They're not exactly your type," I said. "Anthony was always a little bit greasy, a little bit creepy, and a little bit strange."

"A lot a bit strange," Donna said, driving by the doorway once more. "Anthony gave me the shivers."

As much as I didn't want it to be, I was fairly certain the plain, dark-brown door off the alley was where we were headed. "Unfortunately, I think we should park."

"Are you sure you want to do this?" she asked.

"After the day I've had? Not at all. In fact, I want to go back and eat more lasagna and drink the rest of the wine."

Donna put the car in park. "But we should go in. We've got to find someone else who has a motive. We can't let this nonsense go on any longer. I really don't like when people break into your house."

I wrinkled my nose. "Yeah, I'm not a huge fan either."

We both took a deep breath, as well as another sip of the leftover wine Donna had poured into a small flask that read *Bachelorette* in sparkly pink letters on the outside, and gathered up our courage to go inside. Once we stepped out of the car, the chilly night breeze blew leaves between our legs, scratching goose bumps on our skin as they whistled by. It was Halloween weather: trees creaking in the dark evening, black shadows snaking along the edges of the alley, and the promise of an adventure on the other side of the large, mahogany door we stood before.

The door itself was not as plain as it'd looked from the car. Ornate carvings laced the edges, and there were no fewer than nineteen knobs on the outside. Placed in all locations, made of all different materials and all different sizes, it was my best guess which one would get us inside. If any.

"That is one way to make a door more difficult than necessary," Donna said.

"Are they trying to confuse people or keep them out?" I wondered. "Should I turn one?"

Donna shrugged. "Beats me. I'm not into this comic book thing. I saw one of the Spider-Man movies one time."

"More than me. I was a Barbie sorta girl."

"Try one of the doorknobs."

"Why me?" I asked, sizing up too many options.

Donna glared at me.

"Fine. As long as you stay right by me..." I reached out a hand and twisted the knob closest to where a normal door handle would be. A slight zap shocked my fingers, and I leapt backward as if my hand had blown up in flames. My heart pounded, and adrenaline coursed through my veins. I reached out for Donna just as the door swung open from the inside.

I glanced around for my friend, even reaching a hand back to grasp her arm for support, but I snatched nothing but air.

"Donna?" I hissed.

There was a movement behind the trash can next to the door, and I caught a glimpse of Donna's bob behind the lid.

"Donna, get up here." I kept my voice low.

Donna's head emerged hesitantly from behind the bin. I redirected my attention to the doorway, which had opened into a black hole. The door seemed like it'd been opened from a hinge by an invisible hand, but there was no sign of life inside. I couldn't see past the blackness that began an arm's length inside the door and stretched to an infinity. There was no sound except for the shift of Donna rejoining my side.

"Did you see who opened the door?" she asked.

"No," I whispered. "It just kind of popped open. But the handle zapped me."

I shook my hand as if I'd been burned, and Donna reached down to examine it. Apparently she decided I wasn't hurt, because she shook her head and peered into the empty doorway. "This is so freakin' creepy. Should we go in?"

I shrugged, trying not to show my fear despite the creepy crawlies both inside and outside of my body. My skin tingled with anticipation while my guts, currently filled with licorice and lasagna, told me to turn around, go home, and digest in peace.

"I guess we have to." I poked the thick mahogany between the handles, and it swung open a bit more. "It's technically an open door."

"Consider ourselves invited." Donna put one arm around my shoulder, and I welcomed the touch. "You first."

I welcomed the touch a bit less as she gave me a small shove forward, put both her hands around my waist, and cowered behind me as I staggered into the building. We probably looked like a pair of teenagers entering the haunted house at the Minnesota State Fair.

"Oh no. Wall." I crashed into a sturdy piece of cement, which was painted black. In fact, the entrance only appeared to be a black hole, because there was a divider about two feet past the door that filtered us into a tunnel. We could go left or right, but both sides led to dimly lit, small openings that didn't particularly look promising.

"A few signs wouldn't hurt around here," Donna said, straightening up and brushing off her jeans. "A simple arrow or a welcome mat would go a long way."

I gave her a mini-glare as she pretended to be completely nonchalant about pushing me into a dark, scary building and following me at a distance.

"What?" she asked. "I didn't have to come with you."

"That's true," I said, grudgingly. "I appreciate it. I didn't say thank you yet, and I should have."

"Let's get a move on." Donna patted me on the back with a smile. "For Jax's sake. I think he's probably more scared than we are, watching the kids."

"Left or right?"

"Uh...I'll follow you."

I glanced in both directions, went with my gut, and turned left. We followed the dark corridor to the dim light at the end of the tunnel, keeping an eye out for moving shadows, ghosts, and spiders. When we reached the entrance, which was a narrow opening between the two black walls on either side, we paused next to each other.

"Well, this didn't work out." Donna pointed to a sign above the doorway.

Employees Only.

All Regular Folk Forbidden.

"Are we *really* regular folk, though?" I asked.

Donna gave me a crooked eyebrow. "Let's try the other side. Just so happens, turns out your gut feeling was wrong."

"It usually is." I sighed. "Its judgment was clouded by an overload of sugar and caffeine. And a bit of wine."

"That'll do it," Donna said. "Can't make clear judgments on a crappy stomach."

"I didn't say *crappy*. It's quite pleasurable, in fact."

"Yeah, yeah, your sweetness, this way." Donna led the way back down the hall, pausing so that I could go first once we got to the actual entrance. This doorway was a mirror image of the other, except the sign above said *Regular Patrons*.

"Regular, schmegular," I huffed. "These guys sure know how to make their customers feel welcome."

"*Regular* probably has a different meaning at a place like this. I'm not sure their *normal* is quite the same as ours."

I gave Donna a nod of agreement, inhaled a large breath of fresh air, and took a step forward. Donna hesitated, and I attached myself to her wrist, dragging her in behind me. It was a little cold, sure, but I figured we had better chances going as a team.

Safety in numbers, right?

Hopefully two was a big enough number to make a difference.

We stepped around the corner into the mystery room on the other side of the entryway, and I was pleasantly surprised to see that the creepy level wasn't as high as I expected. There had been a small chance someone would be harvesting organs on the other side of the doorway, and I was glad that it didn't seem like the type of place where they'd steal a kidney. At least not in plain sight.

"Who opened the door?" Donna whispered. "We still haven't seen anyone yet."

"Maybe they have a security camera around back. Could be remote control or something. Seems like the type of place they'd get a kick out of playing a little joke on their customers. I mean, the door had about forty knobs on it."

Donna wrinkled her nose. "True. I'm still just a little bit weirded out. Although, it doesn't feel quite as scary now that we're inside."

"I agree. Let's take advantage of the quiet. Maybe if we walk around for a bit, someone will come out and ask us if we need help."

"But do we *want* anyone asking us if we need help?'

I shrugged. *Not particularly.* "We can't ask these books if they've seen Anthony Jenkins. But we could ask a real person."

I gestured toward the rows and rows of books lining the outskirts of the room. It was a decent-sized space, but not huge. It resembled how I imagined a library would look in a private home. The books, however, were thin and brightly colored, their edges crinkly with natural wear and tear. There was a slight musty scent to the room, much like the whiff of well-loved paper one gets when cracking open an old library book that hasn't been touched for ages.

A slight dust coating lined the edges of the shelves, but the place was clearly kept in pristine order. Each and every book was immaculately in place. There were no books lying on the desk in the center of the room, no chairs helter-skelter, and the sliding ladder attached to the bookshelf was firmly pushed against the side.

"Wow, this place is sort of cool." I ran my fingers along the edges of the books, browsing for one I may have been familiar with. Or at least heard of. As I said, I was more of a Barbie girl, not the comic type.

"It almost makes me wish I liked to read." Donna gestured to a glass case, which held the *Ultimate Spider-Man #1* for me to see. "Even you know this one."

"Spider-Man! I've heard of him." I sidled over to Donna. "Maybe I'll pick it up for Harmony. She's not into Barbie—she's a strong, independent woman. She'll appreciate an action book over a doll any day."

"You won't be picking this up for her," Donna said, her eyes wide.

"Why not? She should be encouraged to stimulate whichever part of her brain she—"

"It's like, two hundred dollars."

"She's getting a Barbie," I said, changing my mind at the mention of the price tag.

"Step away from the case." A soft, velvety voice slithered throughout the room.

Donna started, taking a step back.

"Back away...*slowly*." The voice was hardly welcoming, but it wasn't exactly a threat either. Donna stepped back, moving with careful motions so as not to upset the faceless voice coming from the entryway.

The figure wore a thick purple robe that brushed the tops of his shoes as he swayed in place, his face a black hole underneath a hood studded with shimmering crystals. His hands were perched before him, white and scaly in the dim light. The place went from mildly cozy to downright scary in two seconds flat.

I stepped closer to Donna. "Sorry, we were just—"

"Eh, eh, eh...what brings thou here?" The figure waved a hand in our direction.

"We were just browsing..." I gestured at the shelves surrounding us. "All these amazing books. I was looking for a gift for my younger sister."

"Why art thou *really* here?" he asked again.

He moved so little, I wondered if the man was fully alive. I couldn't sit so still, even if I was in a straitjacket.

"To buy a present—" I began again.

"Lies." The man said.

I put a hand on my hip. I was kind of up to my limit with his attitude. "Well, then. Are you a mind reader? Because how do you know I'm not here to buy a book for my sister?"

Donna's mouth fell open.

I'm sorry, I mouthed to her.

"I *know*, because you're not one of the Society. I'm familiar with every individual who appreciates these sacred treasures in our town," he said.

I glanced around at the books, the *treasures*.

"Also, nobody who knows anything about these treasures would call them *books*. Or handle them so carelessly." The man stepped forward and lowered his hood. He cast a disgusted look at Donna.

Donna glanced in my direction, but I was much too distracted by the sight of the man standing before me. Not only did I know him, but I was pretty sure everyone in the town knew him as well.

"Father Olaf?" I asked.

The priest looked mildly annoyed. But even if I hadn't recognized him, the white collar would have given him away. "Yes. Misty. Donna, hello."

"Why did you creep up on us like that?" Donna asked. "Especially if you knew it was us? I mean, I volunteered at the bake sale yesterday, and I've got three kids in the parish school."

"What brings you here?" he asked.

"What brings *you* here?" Donna asked. "And why are you dressed like that? It's a bit...different than your normal robes."

"I'm Merlin." He shifted his eyes, seemingly a bit miffed. "I'm a bit disheartened you can't tell."

"I'm sorry. We definitely should have guessed. Your costume is fantastic," I said.

He looked mildly appeased.

"Why are you dressed as Merlin though?" Donna asked. "What is this place?"

"You should know. You found it. Speaking of—who told you about this place? It's not broadcast in the newspapers, available on the internet, or spoken about by anyone not in the Society."

"I uh...heard it through the grapevine," I said. "I don't really remember."

"Someone is spreading our secrets?" Merlin—or Father Olaf—took a step in my direction.

Reflexively, I took a step back. "I don't think they were purposefully spreading the word. I asked a bit, and it seemed like...uh, hearsay. Nobody really knew much about this place."

"*Who* is spreading our secrets?"

"Why does it matter?" I asked. "If it's just a comic book store, why does it have to be a secret? Wouldn't you want more people to know about it? Then maybe you'd have more customers."

"It is *not* 'just' a comic book store!" Father Olaf raised his voice, speaking in a tone I'd never heard him use at church before. Normally mild-tempered and rather monotone, his inflection today was passionate and energized.

"Aha!" I pointed a finger in his direction. "If it's not *just* a comic book store, then what is it?"

Father Olaf stumbled over his words. "It's a special space for members who appreciate the art of—"

"Have you seen the girls for tonight?" Another familiar voice erupted behind Father Olaf.

Father Olaf appeared immediately agitated. "Quiet. Silence, we have outsiders in the house—"

"Oh, are *you* the girls for tonight?" None other than Alfie appeared behind Merlin, partially shielded due to a nearly frantic Merlin trying to block Alfie's view. Which is probably why the latter didn't recognize us upon first glimpse.

"No, they're—" Merlin began.

Alfie the Cop gasped. "Why aren't you wearing your masks?"

I looked to Donna, who looked as bewildered as I felt. What did the town priest and Alfie the Cop have in common? I couldn't think of a single reason why the two would voluntarily be in the same room except for Christmas Mass. Let alone a musty comic book room.

"They're *not* who you're looking for," Merlin said. It was no use. Alfie bobbed up and down behind him, determined to get a glance at the only customers in the place. They probably didn't see *outsiders* around here too much, based upon how the two were acting.

"Hi, Alfie," I called out, bowing my head and raising a hand in his direction. "It's me."

With a dejected grimace, Merlin dropped his arms, the majestic purple robe dropping to his side.

"Misty? I had no idea you were into cosplay." Alfie stepped around Merlin, his body still in the shadows. To my dismay, his eye held a curious gleam I'd never seen before. "That's very...cool."

"Cosplay?" Donna asked, looking in my direction.

"Don't look at me. I don't even know what that means."

"Costume play," Donna said.

"To the layperson, maybe." Alfie tossed a judgmental glance to Donna. "To *outsiders* like you, I suppose."

"Please, feel free to help me understand what it means then...to an *insider*." I pulled out two chairs at the sparse desk in the center of the room, taking a seat on the first and patting the second for Alfie.

"Not an *insider*." Alfie shook his head sadly. "To the Society."

"The correct term is *kospure*, from Japan," Merlin said.

Alfie nodded. "Let me explain."

He moved forward from the shadow cast by Father Olaf's cape, and to my surprise—and sadness—Alfie was dressed in nothing more than a pair of leggings so tight I feared it was bad for his circulation. A Superman cape hugged his very white, very flabby chest, which was on full display.

I immediately regretted my decision to offer the chair next to me, as Alfie strode confidently into the room, puffing out his chest like an excited little penguin who'd consumed enough food to hibernate for a year.

"Here at the Society, we are avid fans of comics, obviously. But in addition to an appreciation for the physical books, we are *more* than that. We transcend the pages. We bring the characters to life." Alfie proudly pointed to his chest, standing all too close to me, while Merlin tried to disappear in the background. "Superman, you see?"

"I see," I said, wishing I hadn't. I was tempted to shield my eyes, but I needed information, and I didn't want to risk offending the proud penguin who had answers to the questions I needed to ask. "And Father Olaf here, he's part of the Society too?"

"If you mean Merlin, then yes." Alfie gave a smug nod at Father Olaf, who looked as if he would like to disappear into his robe and make this event go away forever. At least from our memories.

"Who else is a part of this Society?" I asked.

"That's classified information," Merlin spoke up from the shadows. "You never told us why you're here."

"On that note, where were *you* tonight between four and eight p.m.?" I asked, my eyes narrowed at Alfie. I couldn't believe I'd forgotten to ask immediately, but in my defense, I'd been a little distracted by the neon-red Speedo he was wearing. The amount of skin showing was very unnecessary.

"What does it mean to you?" Alfie stuck up his nose a bit. "I was at work."

"Were you?" I raised my eyebrow. "Because someone mentioned that you didn't answer a call this afternoon, so...you might want to reconsider your explanation before the cops come talking to you."

"I *am* the cops." Alfie jutted his chin even further out, but I saw his eyes shift nervously to Father Olaf. "Why would they need to talk to me about anything? And especially something you'd know about before me?"

"They'll be talking to you about a break-in at my house." I crossed my arms. "If you don't have a more solid alibi by the time the cops show up, you'll be in a wee bit of trouble, I might think."

"But it wasn't me. Why would I break into your house? Why would you even *think* that?"

I shrugged. "I've been wondering the same thing. But believe me when I say there's already enough evidence to justify asking you a few questions. And don't get any ideas—someone already knows about it, just in case something else should happen to me in the meantime. Someone who can *do* something about it."

"It wasn't me," Alfie said, softer this time.

"All right, fine." I stood up. "Donna, he doesn't want to talk. Let's hit the road."

"But what about..." She paused, giving me googly eyes. I knew that meant "what about the questions we came here to ask?" I shook my head. I had a new, better idea. And it all revolved around Alfie thinking that the main reason I'd come here was to get his alibi and give him a warning.

"I've said all I had to say." I gave Donna a look that said "let's go," and I started walking toward the door.

"Wait," Alfie said, raising a hand. "I was here. I promise you. Don't tell anyone—he can vouch for me." Alfie nodded at

Merlin, who bowed his head as if he was wishing for the zillionth time he'd stayed at home today.

I spun slowly back to face Alfie. "You were here...when you were supposed to be working?"

Alfie looked miserable, and I almost felt bad. Maybe I'd ease up on him after getting the info I needed. "Please don't say anything. I could get in serious trouble."

"Yes, you could." I nodded solemnly. "Why were you here?"

"This costume doesn't make itself." Alfie glanced down at his Superman attire.

He was right. It looked like a five-year-old might have crafted it. At least Merlin's robe looked like it was made from some high-quality fabrics.

"Donna. Phone," I whispered. It was loud enough that I was certain everyone in the room could hear me.

"What do you need a phone for?" Alfie stared at the iPhone Donna handed over, as if it were a bomb instead of a pink-cased cell.

"What do you think I need it for?" I asked, raising it as if I were about to dial a number. What Alfie couldn't see, was that the lock screen was still on, and I could only access the emergency dial and the camera. I chose the latter. It'd probably be faster.

"Don't call, please," Alfie pleaded. "I'll help you. Tell me what you need."

I hesitated, first taking a moment to snap a picture. I'd tried to be subtle, but failed miserably. The flash exploded brightly, and Merlin bent in half, shielding his eyes with his robe sleeves.

"What was that for?" Alfie asked.

"Insurance." I glanced down at the picture of Superman. It would do. It would *more* than do. "You're right. I need information. You can help, or..."

Alfie stared in horror as I waggled the phone back and forth. "You wouldn't."

"It's already in the cloud, so don't you dare try to steal this phone. It'll only make things worse." It was a lie. I didn't have access to any sort of cloud, but he didn't need to know.

"Plus, it doesn't explain why you didn't answer a call this afternoon *or* where you were when my house was broken into today."

"Then why do you need the photo? My life is ruined either way. If I don't have an alibi, everyone will assume I broke into your house—you don't even have anything to steal! If I tell everyone where I was, I'm the weirdo who's into cosplay. Little Lake doesn't understand my type. My life is over."

"But just to be clear, I do have *some* stuff to steal," I added.

Both Alfie and Donna looked at me.

"All right, all right," I said, raising my hands. "I don't. But I understand what you mean when you say Little Lake doesn't understand your type. Do you think it was easy trying to start up my burlesque studio here?"

Alfie fell silent.

"I know how it is to be different," I said softly. I shook my head. "I couldn't even advertise my class in the church bulletin. But listen, Alfie. I don't want to get you in trouble. You help me, and I help get you out of this mess. No blackmail. No alibi. It just goes away."

"How?" he wailed.

I thought for a moment, and even Merlin leaned in a bit closer, his pointy nose pretending not to be paying attention, but his ears clearly listening.

"I thought it was you breaking into my house because I caught you in my office earlier, and you had on this huge backpack. Plus, my fishnet drawer was all askew. When I chased someone away from my home later the same night, it was the logical conclusion to draw. Especially when the intruder drove a cop car away from the scene. He didn't touch anything except for my fishnets again."

Alfie hung his head. "I *know* that I didn't do it, and it *still* looks bad for me from the outside."

"I will vouch for your alibi and not tell anyone the exact details of it. Your name won't be brought up in conjunction with the burglary anymore if you can give me some info on Anthony Jenkins." I put my hands on my hips. "No info, and this picture goes out to Donna's thousand Facebook friends."

"Two hundred," Donna corrected. "There's hardly a thousand people to be friends with in this town."

"*Shh*, that doesn't matter." I shook my head. "Everyone will see it."

Alfie looked up at Merlin with an ashamed look skittering across his face. Father Olaf looked down his nose with that judgmental stare.

"He's...uh, I can't speak about members of the Society." Alfie faltered.

"Fine." I pretended to press a few buttons on the phone that might upload a photo to social media. In reality, I was dialing the number for Pizza Hut on the lock screen and deleting it over and over again.

"Merlin, please, may I?" Alfie asked. "Let me speak of the Society's business just this once."

Father Olaf pondered Alfie's begging for a moment.

"Oh, come on. You're in the background of the picture," I said to Father Olaf. If he wasn't doing anything wrong, then I didn't mind one way or another if the priest enjoyed the comic store. But even so, I didn't think it'd be good for his reputation if word got out.

Merlin looked slightly peeved at my perceived threat. But then he sighed, and as if he'd come to the decision alone, he turned to Alfie. "You may speak of Anthony Jenkins, but only because he disobeyed the rules of the Society before he passed."

"So Anthony was a member of the Society?" I pressed.

Alfie looked up at Merlin, who nodded his head solemnly.

"Yes." Alfie's voice shook. "Anthony was a member of the Society. At least, until...until the very end. He was on his way out."

"Out of what?" I asked.

"The Society. He disobeyed the rules."

"How so?"

"He...he fraternized with one of the *girls*."

I raised my eyebrow at Donna. "You guys have girls in here?"

"That's who you thought we were when you walked in," Donna said. "But wait a second—who *did* you think we were?"

Merlin shook his head, but more out of disappointment than anything else.

"Girls. They come in most nights we're open. There's about four of them on any given night, and they rotate between about eight total." Alfie's cheeks turned pink.

"What do they *do*?" I asked. "Father Olaf...you're not allowed..."

"Merlin never participates," Alfie jumped in. "It's only the rest of us involved in this aspect."

"What activities?" I asked.

"It's not what you think," Merlin said.

"It's cosplay." Alfie stood up, reclaiming the spotlight. "Costume play. The girls come dressed in intricate costumes of various anime, comic book, and other characters. They're paid to play a role."

"What does this have to do with Anthony getting kicked out?"

"Well, the girls...they're paid to be here only for the cosplay role. There's nothing...*intimate* in nature whatsoever," Alfie whispered and looked away from Father Olaf. "They're merely playing their part for the Society."

"Strange," I said. "But go on."

"Anthony, he took it too far. We found out a few weeks ago that he had been fraternizing with one of the girls. That's not allowed."

"Plus, he was married," I added, but at the same time, I felt a trickle of hope. I was getting closer to finding out who might have wanted Anthony dead. "Who was the girl?"

"That's the thing." Alfie hesitated. "The girls are *required* to come in costume with masks covering their faces. We don't know their identities."

"What about the people hiring them? Doesn't that person know?" Donna asked.

"It's cash only. No names."

"How do you get hold of them?" I asked. There had to be a way to track these girls down.

"We send out emails to their Gmail accounts." Alfie held up a hand. "Before you ask, they're all fake ones created for the purpose of this business venture."

"So you know absolutely nothing about these women you invite into your Society to play the role of a superhero?" I couldn't help the incredulousness creeping into my voice.

"It would ruin the ambiance." Alfie crossed his arms. "I don't want to know Wonder Woman bags groceries at Walmart during the day."

I nodded. "I see your point."

Donna sat in the chair next to me. "So you really don't have much to help us out with Anthony, except he was cheating on his wife, which we already knew."

I passed the phone back to Donna, who smiled as she glanced at Alfie's photo. "That's a great pic, isn't it?"

"I have one photo of the girl. Anthony's girl," Alfie burst out. "It's not allowed, I know. I'm sorry Merlin, but she looked incredible as Catwoman."

"Now we're talking," I said.

Alfie slipped his phone out of his pocket, thumbed through a few rows of photos, and eventually held one up to us. There were three people in the photo: Alfie, the girl in question, and the back of Anthony's head. Alfie had a cheesy grin on his face and his arm around the waist of the female, who was at least six inches taller than him in her heels. But the woman's gaze lovingly rested on Anthony.

She had a great body, in Alfie's defense, and made Catwoman look cute. Her costume was skimpy but detailed, her face disguised behind a large Venetian mask.

"She looks a little familiar." I squinted. "It's hard to say though. I've got the best view of her legs, which isn't usually my main focus on women."

"Of course she looks familiar," Alfie snapped. "She's beautiful, and she's a local. You've seen her somewhere, but that's why we don't do names or faces. We don't want to think too hard about who these girls are in real life. Yes, I realize that sounds bad, but if the girl is going home to tuck three kids into bed after a night of cosplay, it takes some of the magic out of it for us. The reason any of us are part of the Society is to suspend our disbelief and believe in the stories once more."

There was something almost endearing about the ferocity with which Alfie spoke. It reminded me of how children defended Santa Claus and the Easter Bunny to nonbelievers.

"Well, I'm sorry to ruin your magic," Donna said. "But this time it's a matter of life or death. If this girl comes back, let us know. We need to talk to her."

"It'll cost you," Alfie said.

"No, it won't." I stood up. "I'm going to tell the cops you were nowhere near my house this afternoon, and they shouldn't even mention a thing about it to you. The second I hear you didn't keep your promise to call us about this girl, I'll be calling the cops and rescinding my story. I'll have a sudden epiphany and remember it clearly."

"That's not fair." Alfie glared at me. "Plus, I am the cops."

"Exactly. Part of the reason you've promised to call us."

"I haven't promised."

"You will." I didn't break eye contact with him. "Come on, Alfie. This doesn't have to be difficult."

"Fine." He glared back at me. "I'll call you if she comes back."

"And I'll do my best to hold her up unsuspiciously until you arrive, Misty," I prompted.

"I promise," Alfie said. "Now, don't you have some kids to go tuck into bed?"

"As a matter of fact, we do." Donna stood up and marched toward the entrance. I followed suit. "Alfie, we'll be in touch."

As Donna and I stepped into the alley, the door behind us snapped shut as quickly as it'd popped open.

"Well, that was an adventure." I smiled.

"Exhilarating. You've bribed a wizard and a cop into giving you information today. I'm not sure if I should be impressed or terrified." Donna's face was flushed and bright. "Now, let's go rescue Jax."

CHAPTER THIRTEEN

───

"Where's Uncle Jax?" Donna called as we entered the house to a suspicious quiet.

A giggle erupted from underneath a couch cushion. "*Shhh*, Mommy. We're playing hide-and-seek. Alec is counting."

"Mmm. Is Jax hiding?" Donna asked to the wiggling pillow in the corner of the couch.

"Yes, Mom. That's how you *play*. Duh."

"Silly me." Donna gave me eyes. She lowered her voice. "He's probably locked in the bathroom with a beer."

I grinned. "I'm gonna go find Harmony. It's about time we get going. Thanks again for everything you've done for me tonight. And since I've been back. I really appreciate it."

"It's no problem at all," Donna said, walking over toward the couch and fake sitting on the cushion. Said cushion emitted a loud fart, and Donna leapt right back up amid gales of laughter from the closet behind the staircase. "My goodness, that is a squeaky couch."

"It's not a couch, Mom," said the closet.

I slipped away, keeping an eye out for partially ajar doors, breathing curtains, and sniffling blankets. I was ninety-five percent certain that I'd identified all of Donna's kids by some sort of movement and/or noise, but Harmony was a very clever hider. I had the guest bedroom upstairs and the bathroom downstairs left to scour before I returned to the kitchen and waited her out.

I pushed open the door to the guest bedroom and muttered a quiet "Gotcha!" A lump of carefully crafted pillows and blankets moved slowly up and down with the rhythm of a person's breathing.

Sneaking forward as quietly as possible, I positioned myself so that I could climb on top of Harmony and tickle her until she squealed. But there were so many pillows on the figure it was hard to tell exactly where my sister's head began and her feet ended. I didn't want to squash her on accident.

"Found you, cutie pie." I leapt onto the bed, throwing aside a pillow and diving in for the tickles.

But instead of a tiny child's body, my hands came into contact with a solid, firm chest with way more muscle than belonged on a nine-year-old body. And definitely way more chest hair, which I could feel through the soft fabric of his shirt.

I stumbled backward, a bit surprised. Though now that I thought about it, I hadn't factored Jax into my number count when I'd noted all the other hiders. I'd figured he was, as Donna suggested, locked in the downstairs bathroom sipping his beer and reading the paper.

Before I completely tumbled from the bed, two muscular arms snaked out from under a flowery blanket and drew me back into to the fluffy pile.

"Can it, or they'll find us," Jax whispered, his breath hot against my ear. Despite the layers of blankets and pillows and whatever else he'd piled on the bed, a chill coursed through my veins, goose bumps pricking my legs.

"You take your hide-and-seek seriously," I said.

"I don't like to lose, and your sister is a genius at this game."

"She learns from the best."

"Really?" Jax put his hand behind my neck and pulled me in close. "Does the best keep yapping for the whole game so she can get caught?"

I closed my mouth but hissed through barely parted lips. "I'm not *yapping*."

"You're pricking me."

"With what?" I looked down. My leg had become entangled with his in the messy pile of sheets and limbs. "*Ooops. It's not my fault I didn't have time to shave today, since someone broke into my house and interrupted my shower.*"

"Keep it down. Keep it down." Jax pressed a finger to my lips. "Let's not sabotage the entire game."

I rolled my eyes, but I stopped talking. A part of me didn't want the game to end. After the last couple of days, I'd been looking over my shoulder left and right, not sure which shadows to run from and which to confront. The privacy of my home and my studio had been shattered, as well as the hopefulness I'd felt when I opened the studio. But the disappointment and fear disappeared underneath the ancient, musty comforter forming a private tent around our bodies.

Jax pressed to me, one of his arms still lazily draped over my shoulders, the other brushing against my waist, though I was certain it wasn't on purpose. His fingers were inches away from the sensitive skin below my belly button, and for a second I could pretend that our hearts had never been broken due to an impossibly timed love.

We could have been two adults, married now with kids of our own playing hide-and-seek, instead of strangers brought together out of necessity. I cleared my throat, trying to shake the old memories and cherish the new.

"Are you okay?" Jax asked. The arm around my back pulled me in tighter.

I nodded. I wasn't quite ready to speak.

"Good. I hear the seeker in the hall. *Shhh.* Come closer."

The command for silence was a welcome one. I nestled into the crook of his arm, and it twisted my heart that I fit just as perfectly now as I had ten years before. Except now, this wasn't my arm-crook to cuddle in—a fact I needed to remember.

"He skipped over us for now. We're good." Jax's grin shone through as if he were a child himself. It warmed my insides to see he hadn't lost his playful side despite years on the force, having seen what I assumed were some pretty bad things over the course of the past decade. "How was your night?"

"It was good. But how was yours? Thanks for watching the kids. That was really sweet of you."

"That's what uncles do." Jax smiled. "Plus, it's been a while since I got a challenging round of hide-and-seek in. Does a body good."

I laughed. Jax covered my mouth with his hand, and we both lost it, cracking up into our respective pillows, his hand firmly pressed against my lips.

When we calmed, he made eye contact with me, pushing up the edge of the covers so we could grab a breath of fresh air. The meeting of our gazes lasted for only an instance, a brief crash of happy and sad that was extinguished as he let the cover drop, and we were plunged into darkness once more.

"They didn't find anything at your house," Jax said. "Nathan called and said that none of the men on the scene seemed suspicious—and nothing in the house was off, so far as they could tell. Unless, of course, your sock drawer is missing some things."

"I wouldn't know."

"Neither would I." I could feel Jax's smile more than I could see it. "Apparently you have fifty-one fishnet stockings."

"Hmmm. Nice of them to count."

"Why not stop at fifty? Do you really need that extra one?"

"Very funny, haha." I poked him in the chest, then ran my prickly leg up his until he flinched.

"Ow! You're a madwoman."

"Stop poking around in my underwear drawer."

"We're just being thorough." Jax's voice dropped to a more somber tone. "Speaking of…things don't look good for Alfie. He missed a call this afternoon, even though he was signed into the log. He wasn't on a break, but he was unresponsive for about an hour before he returned and filed a speeding ticket, which was a bullshit ticket anyway. The guy wasn't even speeding."

"It wasn't Alfie," I said.

"Excuse me?"

"It wasn't him who broke into my house."

"Misty, I don't know what happened to you at that comic book store—I've heard some weird stuff goes on there, so if they put a spell on you or something, if they threatened you…"

"It's nothing like that." I placed a hand on Jax's shoulder, the solid bicep not lost on me. "Nothing happened, but I had a chat with Alfie, and he has an alibi. He didn't do it. Just let it drop."

"I can't let it drop. That's not in my job description. Not to mention, you're still a suspect in an unsolved murder. No offense, but your *word* doesn't mean a whole lot to me right now."

His comment stung, but I ignored it. "It wasn't Alfie."

Jax stared at me.

"It wasn't him," I said. "So drop it."

"Who else has access to a cop car that would harm you? Or steal from you?"

"That's what we need to find out, isn't it?" I turned my head away slightly, but Jax raised a hand and tipped it right back, his fingers firm on my chin. "What?"

"I don't like when people are messed with. Especially you. Tell me what's going on."

I sighed. Jax held up a finger as footsteps padded past us in the hall, Alec screaming that he couldn't find Harmony.

When Jax dropped his finger, I resumed. "Alfie has an alibi for the time during which my house was broken into. It's a little bit embarrassing, but it's been backed up by a very reliable source."

"Who is this source?"

"I can't tell you that either."

"Misty…" Anger steeped beneath the surface of his voice.

"Listen. It's a person in a position of this town that…could be compromised if their whereabouts during the time of the alibi came out. I talked to both of them, and I believe both of them. This is coming from someone—me—who *wanted* us to believe it was Alfie. I *wanted* to believe this was all about an intruder wanting a sniff at my stockings. Frankly, I'm disappointed it wasn't. I was getting used to the idea of having a stalker."

"This isn't funny, Misty."

"Gallows humor, haven't you heard of it?"

"Why should I not question Alfie right this very minute?"

"Because he promised, along with this other source, to help me find a person that has information about Anthony Jenkins. And I need information about Anthony Jenkins to clear my own name."

Jax didn't say much, probably because he was the one who'd prompted me to clear my name in the first place.

"Give me a few days, Jax. They're going to call me when this person shows up—this person that has information on Anthony. If nothing happens, or if this person is a dead end, it's free range, and I'll tell you everything you need to know. I'm an open book."

"Three days."

"Five."

"Three."

"Okay, fine. Thank you." I paused. "I appreciate that."

"My circumstances are that you call me, which requires getting a phone, the second you hear from Alfie or your source. I want to know when you meet this *person*. Got it? No going alone."

"Maybe alone."

"I want to know where you are so I can remain a safe distance away."

"You're infuriating."

"Take the deal."

"Fine."

"Gotcha!" shouted a small voice. Jax and I flinched as tiny limbs started jumping on top of the bed. "Double whammy."

We sat up.

"Nice work, Alec." Jax held out a hand for a high five. "What gave us away?"

"She was yelling at you." Alec pointed to me.

"I was not," I said.

Jax raised his eyebrows at me, a grin creasing the laugh lines around his eyes.

"Whatever, you won," I grumbled.

"Did not," Alec retorted. "I can't find Harmony."

"I'm here!" Another voice shouted. This one came from under the bed.

"You've been under there this whole time?" Jax asked as Harmony slithered out from underneath the bed.

"Yep." Harmony grinned. "You guys are silly. By the way, what's a stalker? And why would he want to smell socks?"

"Ew," Alec said.

"Totally gross," I agreed, staring over their heads at Jax. "Time to head out, Harmony."

"Can we please sleep over?" Harmony bobbed up and down.

"No, not tonight, honey," I said. "I gotta get you home to Mom."

"I can call her and ask her to stay," my sister begged.

"I don't have a phone."

"I do," said Jax. He pulled a cell out of the jeans riding low on his waist. "Go ahead."

"What do you think you're doing?" I crossed my arms.

"There's no way you want to sleep in a house that was broken into hours ago. Sleep in this room." Jax gestured toward the destroyed bed. "In fact, I think you've already made yourself comfortable."

I wrinkled my nose. "I'll be fine. I lived in Los Angeles for ten years, and I made it out alive. I had my apartment broken into, car window smashed, creepy notes left under my door—I survived."

"I know." Jax's face was solemn.

My next retort faltered on my tongue. "I'll be okay."

"Just stay. I insist. Honestly, Donna won't even be able to tell. She's got enough kids in this place, you'll fit right in."

"Thanks for that."

"It's true." Jax winked. "Except even the kids don't eat Froot Loops for nine out of ten meals in a week."

"Oh, thanks, Mom," Harmony said, hanging up the phone and handing it back to Jax. "Mom doesn't care. She's out on a date, so she won't be home til late anyway."

"Did I hear someone talk about staying overnight?" Donna appeared in the doorway. "This room's all yours. Stay, Misty. You and Harmony can have a sleepover in the bed. Plus, it's late. You don't want to walk home, and it's irresponsible to be in that place without a phone right now anyway."

The idea of a warm bed was pretty appealing. The wind whistling outside whispered against the window, telling me to stay, warning me against the chilly outdoors and the shadows slipping through the night.

"All right." I ruffled Harmony's hair. I didn't say it aloud, but there was also the implied promise of breakfast that wasn't cereal. "We'll stay. Twist my arm."

"Yippee!" Harmony leapt up and pumped a fist. No sooner had she landed than she darted off to play with the other kids.

"Don't get any ideas," I called after her. "Bed soon."

There was no answer. Oh well. It'd do us both good to have some fun and to take our minds off things. Mine was heavy with the weight of the comic shop findings, the worry I didn't have a phone or a car, the fear my life would collapse into a bigger mess than it already had.

But the one thing I did have going for me was a pretty kick-ass friend. I couldn't ask for a better sidekick than Donna. And as I glanced up at her, hoping she knew how grateful I was, I couldn't help but feel a surge of warmth toward Jax too. Maybe we could be friends after all. Just friends, of course.

"I'll grab you some blankets." Donna disappeared from the room, leaving Jax and me together in a silence that couldn't seem to decide if it was awkward or friendly.

"Well, thanks," I said.

"For?"

"Checking out my house, watching the kids…all that stuff."

"It's my job."

I couldn't tell if Jax was reminding himself or me. Either way, his point was clear. *It wasn't personal.*

"I'll see you." I shrugged.

"I'm just down the block if you need anything. I expect a phone call if you hear anything about…anything."

I smiled. "Deal."

Jax leaned in, and I opened myself up for a one-armed side hug. But Jax pushed past and brushed a quick kiss against my forehead before striding out the door without looking back.

CHAPTER FOURTEEN

———

I woke up cuddled with Harmony on a bed full of blankets and comforters, decorated with enough pillows to outfit a furniture store. I stroked her blonde hair gently, remembering one of the main reasons I'd ended up back in Little Lake. It had been a culmination of my grandmother's passing, inheriting the house, and feeling like I was missing out on my baby sister's life. Then, there'd been the ACL incident, which had knocked me off the dancing stage for the foreseeable future.

"Misty, are you awake?" Donna poked her head into the bedroom.

I nodded, lifting a finger to my lips so we wouldn't disturb the peacefully sleeping Harmony.

"C'mere," Donna half whispered, half mouthed.

I slipped out of bed and padded over to the doorway.

"Is everything okay?" I whispered, shutting the door behind me.

"This was under the door."

I glanced at the envelope in Donna's hand. There was one word on the front of it.

My name.

"Did you see who left..." I asked.

Donna shook her head no before I finished the question. "Do you want me here when you open it?"

I hesitated. *Yes*, because I wanted the support. *No*, because I wanted the privacy to feel sad or upset or scared alone. "Of course."

Slipping my finger under the lip of the envelope, I peeked up at Donna.

Her face was turning pinker by the second.

"Breathe," I instructed.

A whoosh of air escaped from her lungs. "Oh, that's better. I was too anxious to see who it's from."

I finished popping open the envelope and sliding out a flimsy sheet of paper. It was folded in half and looked like it had music and lyrics on one side. Almost like a church hymnal.

"Father Olaf?" Donna guessed.

I shrugged. Flipping it over, I read the handwriting squashed between a few lines of prayer. "Confession is at nine a.m."

Donna's eyes were wide as she met my gaze. "No, it's not. Confession is at four p.m. What do you think that means?"

"I'm assuming he wants me to meet him at church."

"That's…that's a little odd. I'm not sure if you should go," Donna said.

"But what if he knows something he didn't want to say in front of Alfie last night? I have to go."

"You don't have to go."

"Yes, I do." I gave Donna my most determined stare.

"Then I'll go with you."

"No, Donna. No. Thank you for everything you've done and all your help and support, but you have a candy store to run. Kids to feed and clothe and water—or whatever it is you do to keep them alive and happy and adorable. This is my problem."

"I want to help." Donna reached over and squeezed my hand.

"You will. You are. You already have."

"I'll take Harmony home. I'll feed her and get everything ready. It's no problem," she said.

"Are you sure?" I felt bad—she'd already done so much.

"Yes, of course. That's how I'll help you. It's eight fifteen already. You've got to hurry. Stop by Jax's, though, and let him know. Maybe he can drop you off on his way to work."

"I'll check."

"Aww, honey. This will all be over soon." She clasped my face in her hands, assessing my expression.

I did my best to be cheery. But really I was wondering if going one-on-one into a confessional based upon an unsigned, hand-delivered note was the best idea I'd have today.

* * *

I kissed Harmony good-bye, and she was more than overjoyed to be spending the morning with the other kids. They were licking the frosting off Toaster Strudels when I thanked Donna once more and dipped out the front door.

It was a short walk to Jax's place a few doors down. I wasn't sure that I'd want to be neighbors with all my siblings—it was a little bit too close for comfort to me. But, I had to admit, the convenience was nice. He functioned not only as a built-in babysitter but a person to call if Donna's car broke down, or one of her kids was sick, or any number of things. It wasn't until I'd moved away to Cali that I started noticing the positives of being close to family. Plus, it was much less lonely.

I reached the front of Jax's modest place, lost in my thoughts, and I barely noticed the blonde bob bouncing down the steps as I turned up the sidewalk into his front lawn.

"Oh, hey, Misty. What are you doing here?" Sarah flashed a grin in my direction, but confusion was written over her face.

"Oh, Sarah—hi." She'd caught me off guard, and it took me a moment to figure out why she was leaving Jax's place.

The realization that she'd probably slept over and was heading to work hit me. "Oh, I was, uh, looking for Jax. I had to tell him something—police business—uh, do you know where he is?"

Sarah hesitated at my babbling. "He's at the station."

"Oh."

"Do you need something?" She cast a gaze beyond me, as if in a bit of a hurry.

"I just had to tell Jax about something..."

"Do you want me to pass on a message?"

"No, no, that's all right. I'll just...you said he's at the station?"

"Yeah. He's working," she repeated.

"Do you know what time it is, by chance?" Without a phone, and without wearing a watch, I was clueless.

Sarah clicked her phone on. It's eight twenty-eight. Are you sure everything's okay?"

"Yeah, I just have somewhere to be. Thanks anyway." I turned and headed down the path, trying to calculate whether or not I could make it to the station before I hit the church.

No, I decided. I barely had enough time to make it to the church from here—it was a solid two mile walk, so I'd have to hustle.

"Do you need a ride?" Sarah called from the doorway.

I turned around. She'd moved back toward Jax's house and had a key in the lock. *She already had a key?*

I pushed away the small hint of jealousy and smiled. "No, I'm okay, thanks."

"Honestly, I just have to grab something from upstairs. If you don't mind waiting a sec, I can drop you off in town, or at the station, when I head out." She paused. "About what I said on the phone the other night…I hope I didn't upset you."

"No, no. You have every right to be nervous about helping me out. I shouldn't have asked."

"No, I want to help. I do. A real friend would be there for you when you need them." She gave a weak smile. "I didn't do a great job of that so far."

"It's better this way—believe me. Once everything is cleared, we can hang out. I'm just going to walk down there. I have time."

"Let me give you a ride to the station. I insist. I want to make up for not rescheduling the comic store trip with you."

"Oh, I already went there, so it's not even an issue," I said brightly.

Sarah raised her eyebrows. "Wow! You went last night then?"

I smiled. "Yep. You didn't miss anything."

"Hm. Tell me about it in the car. I insist on taking you."

I hedged a bit. I didn't want to put anyone else in danger more than I already had. "Is it out of your way?"

"Not at all. I have extra time. I was even considering stopping by the station just to surprise Jax and say hi this morning anyway. It's no trouble at all."

"In that case, I'd really appreciate it." I headed back up the pathway and followed Sarah into Jax's house.

It was clear a bachelor lived here, but the attempts to make it a little more homey were obvious, even though it was more of a patchy attempt at this point. A picture of Jax and Sarah sat on the entryway table, but judging by the lack of dust or fingerprints on it, the frame was a new one. A purse lounged in the chair beside the door, and a woman's jacket—probably Sarah's—hung in the open entryway closet.

"Nice flowers." I smiled and pointed to the sunflowers next to the photo of her and Jax. "I see you've added a nice feminine touch to the place."

"You know, *guys*," Sarah said. "They'd leave all the windows shut and drapes pulled if it weren't for us. I like to brighten the place up a bit. Or at least I try."

Sarah dashed upstairs, calling down that she'd only be a second.

I poked around the entryway, trying to get a feel for the way Jax lived these days. The walls were fairly bare, the carpets and rugs nondescript but classy. He lived simply, I assumed, based on the lack of clutter on most surfaces and the minimum amount of furniture in his home.

He had a couch and a television in the sitting room, which I could see from the entryway, and a kitchen next to it that had only the necessary appliances and a coffee machine on the counter. One mug hung from the drying rack. *Sarah's?*

"Ready?" Sarah's voice jolted me back.

"Yeah. I'm ready. Thanks again."

Once we were strapped into Sarah's sporty little car, cute and zippy, she headed in the direction of the station. "Sorry again that I bailed on you last night. I didn't know they were closed today."

"It's no problem. Of course you didn't know." I relaxed in the passenger seat, grateful for saving my feet the extra steps to the station.

"Yeah, still…"

"My feelings aren't hurt. And I really appreciate you giving me a ride. We're all good." I smiled at Sarah, and I was surprised to realize my feelings were genuine. My grudge was starting to fade. It was a nice change.

"How was it though?" Sarah's eyes twinkled. "Did you find out anything?"

"Not too much. Apparently Jenkins was a member there—they're very into cosplay. Do you know what that is?"

"Costume play. Yeah, I flew out to San Diego for Comic-Con once. It's pretty fun."

"Oh, wow. I never knew. But anyway, they were all dressed up like characters, and some of the people who were there, you'd be *real* surprised at."

"Hunh," Sarah said. "Like who?"

"Actually, I promised I wouldn't say." I bit my lip, already backtracking. I probably shouldn't have told Sarah the details, especially since I hadn't mentioned them to Jax. "I'm sorry, I've said too much already."

"Anything about Anthony?"

"Not really." I glanced out the window, wanting to ditch the rest of her questions. "Anyway, this is great here. Thanks so much for the ride."

Sarah nodded.

"Were you going to say hi to Jax?" I asked, getting out of the car. I looked back through the window. Her hands still firmly gripped the wheel, and she didn't look like she was moving anywhere too soon.

"No, I'm gonna get going, I think." She gave me a small smile. "Good luck!"

She was off as I raised my hand to wave good-bye.

I didn't think about Sarah anymore as I headed inside the station. My mind was already onto other things, namely finding Jax, telling him about the note, and getting over to the confessional by 9:00 a.m., which was now in twenty-two precious minutes, based on the clock on the wall.

"Alfie," I nodded. He was manning the front desk. *Of course he would be*—today was the day the comic shop was closed. What else would he be doing?

I was proud of myself for having enough restraint to hold back a minor smirk as Alfie blushed. "Misty, how can I help you?"

"I'm looking for Jax."

"For what, if I may ask?"

I leaned on the counter. "You may not ask."

Alfie's ears reddened, and he looked a little bit like a teakettle that was just about to boil. I wouldn't have been surprised if he started steaming. "Fine, then. In his office."

He thumbed me down a hallway straight behind him, and I took off, scanning for the name plaque that would tell me I'd reached my destination.

"Look who it is." I whirled to face the familiar voice behind me.

"Jax. I must have missed your office."

"It's not marked." Jax pointed to what may have been a broom closet. There *was* a name plaque, but in my defense it wasn't what I'd been looking for. Instead of white block letters, the name Jax was spelled J-A-C-K-S in color crayon, with snowmen dancing around the letters and a yellow exclamation mark that looked like a hot dog. Clearly a gift from one of Donna's kids.

"That's a beautiful nameplate."

"That's why I leave it up." Jax grinned. "What can I do for ya?"

"I got a letter this morning."

Jax looked up and down the hallway, his grin melting into a mask that intersected on curious and concerned. "Come in."

The interior of his office was not much better than the broom closet I'd initially thought it to be. Two mismatched, raggedy chairs sat on opposite sides of a plain metal table. Papers were spread on his desk, semi-organized to him probably but chaotic to an average bystander. A computer perched against a stand to his left, and there was a tiny, college-style refrigerator on the other side of the room.

"Something to drink?" Jax asked. "Sorry for the cramped quarters. I prefer to spend my time on the streets instead of sitting behind a desk."

"Someone slipped this under my door." I slid the sheet of paper over to where Jax leaned against his desk.

He picked it up and read the message quickly, his eyes flicking up toward me before going back to the paper, presumably to read it again.

"Does Donna know about this?" he asked.

I nodded. "She woke me up this morning. Found it under the door. She offered to take care of Harmony so I could tell you about it, but you weren't..."

"Weren't at home."

"Right. Sarah dropped me off here."

Jax cast a curious gaze at me, but I was glad he didn't press further. It wasn't *only* that I didn't want to talk about it. I mean, it was partially true that I didn't want to acknowledge the fact he had a girlfriend, but we also didn't have time to chat this morning.

"I need to get to the church. Can you drop me off?"

"I'm coming with you."

"You're not." I stood up. "I came here on good faith that you wouldn't interfere. You wanted to keep abreast of this case, and I'm doing you a favor by letting you know beforehand."

"Are you?" Jax took a step forward, lightly clasping his hand around my bicep. "Or are you scared out of your mind that some creep might be waiting in there for you with a gun?"

I hadn't realized I'd been holding my breath, but it all whooshed out of me when he pulled me even closer to him. I glanced everywhere but into his eyes, though I didn't fool him.

"You're scared, aren't you?" Jax tipped my chin to look into his eyes. "Tell me yes, or else you're crazier than I thought."

I glared into his eyes. "Yes. I'm scared. I'm terrified. But I need to go in there alone."

"Let me come with. I'll stay in the shadows."

"Will you?" I glanced up at him, my neck tilted backward because my face was already so close to his. "Do you promise? If this is the chance I have to figure out who killed Anthony and you blow it..."

"I promise. Let's go. We can talk more in the car."

CHAPTER FIFTEEN

———

We didn't talk more in the car. On the contrary, we were silent. The church was only a mile or so away, and we made quick time. As we drove past the church, Jax showed no signs of stopping.

"Are you going to let me out eventually?" I asked.

Jax gave me a non-amused look.

"Where will you park that your car won't be seen?" We'd taken his civilian car and not the cruiser, but still, the chances of someone recognizing Jax's car parked alone in the church lot at 9:00 a.m. were high.

"Get out here," Jax instructed. "I know a spot. I'll text you when I park, and that's your cue to go in. *Do not* go in before. Do you understand me?"

Oh, crap. I was supposed to have gotten a phone this morning. Jax either forgot I didn't have a working one, or he assumed I'd reactivated my plan like he'd ordered. But with the appearance of the note, I'd completely forgotten. "Yes, of course. You have my number?"

"Courtesy of Donna."

"Great." Giving him my number wouldn't have been a full-fledged lie. My number *was* the same, it just wasn't functional.

"Good." He put a hand on my shoulder. "Be careful in there. Call me when you go in. Leave your phone on so I can hear what's going on. Say if you need something, and I'll come right in."

"Thank you." I tried for a smile. "I'm sure it'll be fine."

Jax's grim expression didn't harbor a lot of hope through his window as he rolled away down the street.

I took a moment for a few deep breaths, begged my heart to beat a little bit softer, and eventually gave up trying to calm myself. Moving closer toward the church, I saw no signs of Jax. I also didn't see a sign of anyone else, but that didn't mean much. If it was Father Olaf like I expected, he most likely walked here. And if it was someone who didn't want to be discovered…well, the person wouldn't leave a car parked directly out front either.

I didn't have a watch or a phone, so I was a bit clueless on the time. I knew it'd been 8:54 when I'd gotten out of Jax's car, which left six minutes before I had to meet the mystery guest. *Had five minutes passed already?* It easily could have. It could've been ten, for all I knew. Or one. Time was hard to judge when my adrenaline was cranking at a hundred miles an hour—it felt like the world had stopped completely.

I took a few quick steps behind a nearby trash bin and glanced around. The place was a graveyard. A slight breeze carried a few miscellaneous napkins across the front lawns and ruffled the breezes of the now-browning roses out front. The needles on the evergreen tree beside the door whispered a quiet warning, clicking against one another as if they knew of a danger that waited inside.

Goose bumps pricked my arms, and after one more quick scan of the yard and no sign of Jax, I figured he was probably already in place somewhere. He had years of training and experience. I kept telling myself that it was a *good* thing I couldn't see him. That meant the bad guys couldn't see him either.

Time to go, Misty. I gave myself a quick, private pep talk that I didn't ever want repeated. There was definitely some bargaining with God in there and some promises for a lot of prayers to be said.

During my pep talk, I'd crept slowly toward the large front doors of the church. I put a hand on one big knob and pulled. To my surprise, the door swung open easily and silently, and I was inside before I had a chance to think further about it.

"Hello?" My voice, though muted, echoed through the large chamber.

The carpets of the church were royal red, the pews completely empty. A few candles flickered at the front along the altar. There were a few cornucopias and fall wreathes with fresh leaves and flowers on display as decorations. Under different circumstances, I would've described the place as regal. Today, however, it seemed cavernous and dark.

The confessional was at the far back, draped in a purple cloth. It was a small room, one side for the priest, the other for the confessor, and a divider in between. I pulled back the purple cloth and sat down.

There was a slight movement on the other side of the divider and the sounds of shifting clothes, though I couldn't tell who was there.

"Hello?" I whispered.

"Misty," a throaty voice croaked. "You?"

"Yes, it's me. Is that you, Father Olaf?"

"I have something to confess," he said in answer.

"We're on the wrong side of the confessional, then," I said.

There was a slightly awkward silence. "I know something about Anthony Jenkins that most people don't."

"What is it?" I pressed a hand to the divider. *Please. Please be something helpful.* I just needed information to clear my name from a crime I didn't commit.

There was a long, long silence, and I thought for a second he'd gotten up and left.

"Father," I hissed. "Father, please. What is it?"

Father Olaf cleared his throat. "I...I don't know if I can say."

"Why did you call me here then?"

"I want to tell you, but it was something Anthony asked me to keep a secret."

I imagined Merlin shuddering in his purple hat. "I won't say a word about it. I promise you. But if it's information I can use to clear my name...please. Anthony is dead, and I still have a life ahead of me. Please, help me."

"But—"

"Please. I won't tell anyone. What did Anthony say?"

"I...I don't even know if it was anything. He was mumbling and...and I could smell alcohol on his breath. He wasn't making much sense."

"Would you say there was a chance he was drunk?"

"A very high probability. In fact, I had to drive him home that night. Or rather, to the comic store so he could sober up before he went back to his wife. He stumbled into her one night after evening Mass and started spewing nonsense. I think it was almost as if he wanted to confess something, but it was difficult to understand him."

"Well, he didn't confide in you during confession, so you're not breaking any rules by telling me. Please, if there's something that will help, I need to know. For both my sake and for Anthony's sake. I need to find who killed him."

A long sigh escaped. "I suppose. However, you received this information from an anonymous source, and it will never be tied back to my name."

"I understand."

"Anthony recently came into money. A *lot* of money. Someone had a motive to kill him, but I still don't know who it was."

"Where did he get the money?"

"Inherited it when his grandmother died. They were estranged, but for some reason she left him a large chunk of her rather expansive estate."

"Who is the money left to?" I asked.

"His wife. He discussed the will with me. It was signed one day before he died."

I gulped. "Mrs. Jenkins?"

There was silence. "You must go."

"Thank you, Father," I whispered, just as I heard the soft click of the confessional door close.

I continued to sit and seriously contemplate sneaking out the back door of the church in order to avoid Jax's probably unhappy face at the sight of mine. But I figured it wasn't really worth it. He'd find me sooner or later, and it'd only get worse if I snuck off. Also, I kind of wanted a ride to Mrs. Jenkins's house. I strolled out the front door of the church, looking around. I gave a low whistle, but everything was still.

"Jax?" I hissed.

Nothing.

Dang, maybe he hadn't come, anyway. Maybe he'd kept right on rolling down the street.

I gave it a few more seconds before deciding that it'd be faster for me to hoof it back to the station on foot, rather than wait around for a ride I wasn't even sure was coming. Maybe he'd gotten distracted by a more urgent call and had forgotten me.

I felt a twinge of hurt at the thought, but I pushed it away. He'd done a lot to help me recently, and I was the one who'd insisted on going in alone in the first place. He'd offered to come with me, and I said no.

"Doesn't feel good when things don't go according to plan, does it?" Jax stepped from an alleyway next to the church, nearly giving me a heart attack in the process.

I pressed a hand to my chest. "You scared me."

"That's how I felt when I realized you'd gone inside without my signal."

I moved uncomfortably from foot to foot. I wasn't sure which story I'd be better off telling him—that I'd not gotten a new phone or that I'd blatantly disobeyed his request.

"You didn't get your plan activated, did you?"

"Not a hundred percent," I said, my eyes downward.

"Not even twenty percent." Jax stepped forward. "This is getting dangerous, you without a phone."

"I'll get one."

"Do you need a ride to the telephone store? I'll drop you off on the way to the station. I'll see you inside myself. Handcuff you to the register."

"Sure. I'd love a ride. Thanks, though I don't appreciate the sarcasm." I smiled. "But one request first. How about a ride to Mrs. Jenkins's house?"

"I'm not sure you're in a position to make requests. What happened in there?" Jax had started to walk toward his car with me following close behind, but he stopped abruptly.

"It was...someone with inside knowledge of Anthony Jenkins."

"Someone from the comic shop."

"Yes."

"Someone whose name you refuse to tell me."

"Uh, sort of." I winced, trying to forget that I'd let a few details slip when I'd talked to Sarah. Jax looked rather threatening at the moment, which almost made me change my mind. But I held out. "I promised I wouldn't say a word."

Jax sighed. "Do you trust this information?"

"I do. I really do. It's from a reliable source."

"Well?" Jax picked up his pace.

I jogged behind, climbing into the passenger side of his car before I began speaking. "Apparently Anthony had recently come into a lot of money. Some estranged grandma left it to him. It was a surprise to everyone, I guess. But it was enough money for a motive."

"Which is where Mrs. Jenkins comes in…because it was left to her?"

"You guessed it. Whatever the exact situation, she would get the money if he died. And get this—the will was signed *one day* before he died. It was like she killed him just after the ink dried. So tacky," I said.

"If she'd waited a week, it would've been less tacky?" Jax asked.

I frowned. "You know what I mean."

"If there really is a will, this could be our motive. I wonder why we haven't heard about it yet."

"Well, it sounded pretty new. I'm not sure how many people know about it. My contact heard it through…other channels."

Jax nodded thoughtfully. "Let's pay her a visit. We can get your phone after."

I smiled. "Thank you. I appreciate you driving me around."

"My taxi services don't come cheap." Jax raised an eyebrow.

I blushed. "I'll owe you one."

We drove in silence for a few minutes. "So Father Olaf is into the cosplay stuff, huh? I'm not totally surprised."

"How did you find out?" I asked, my mouth dropping. Recovering quickly, I tried to backtrack. "I mean, what makes you think that?"

"The fact he walked out the front doors of the church thirty seconds before you, looking more than a little flustered."

"Don't say *anything*," I threatened. "Or else."

"Or else what? I won't get this mysterious big 'thing' you owe me for the ride?"

"Yes. Exactly."

The jokes died down as we pulled up to Mrs. Jenkins's place. It was just as dreary as I remembered it, and I felt no warmth at the thought of going in and having another interaction with the crazy woman who probably killed her husband.

"Mrs. Jenkins didn't bring up any sort of money issues between her and Anthony," Jax said. "I wonder why she didn't bring it up. She'd have to know we'd find out about it."

"She probably figured that nobody knew about it. And she probably *didn't* want people to know about it because it gives her a motive and points the smoking gun right at her. Maybe she was just biding her time so she could claim the money later, once I'm all locked up in prison."

Suddenly indignant, I pointed a finger at Jax. "That's probably why she signed up for my class. So she could keep an eye on me. That witch."

"Whoa, watch the language," Jax said. I couldn't tell if there was a subtle wink in there or not. Either way, I was steamed. Mrs. Jenkins had been trying to pin this thing on me the whole time, and I'd been teaching her how to *shimmy*!

"Let's go in. I want to have a chat with my student," I said, opening the car door.

Jax was already on the phone, muttering something about wills and warrants and all that sort of legal stuff.

I shut the door as he got out of the car.

"We have to be careful about this," Jax said. "We'll go inside—yes, I'm coming with you." He didn't stop at my *please don't come with* face. "But let's feel out the situation. I still haven't actually seen a copy of this will, and your source is a faceless man who you won't reveal."

I shrugged.

"So let's see if we can get her to admit that she omitted some details about the will. Deal? Don't go in accusatory. Let me do the talking."

I harrumphed, but I didn't disagree. As mad as I was, I kept reminding myself that at the end of the day what I really wanted was the real murderer in jail so I could go freely about my business.

"Do you have a gun?" I asked as we approached the door together.

Jax simply looked at me.

"Okay, okay," I said. "Just checking. She had a pretty big knife on her last time we came in here."

Jax exhaled a huge breath, and I thought he might've even considered doing the sign of the cross. Instead, he knocked.

I looked up at him expectantly, his face grim, eyes set straight forward. He made a good cop, I had to admit. He listened and was kind in general, stern and serious when necessary. I bet he made a great team leader. Not only because people liked him but also because he was out on the street doing the footwork with everyone else.

I knocked again.

Jax's cheek twitched a bit, but he didn't say anything.

When I knocked a third time, he put his hand over mine.

"Let's come back," he said, not removing his hand.

"No. What if she sees it's you, and she's hiding in there?" I pounded again. "We can't let her get away."

"I don't think she's home right now."

"But her car's here." I pointed to a beat-up truck that Anthony used to drive around. It was originally white, but the paint was peeling so badly it looked more like a cow.

"Maybe she went for a walk. It's not like this is the largest town in the universe."

"I think we should go in."

"Believe it or not, I can't just break down anybody's door that I want."

"But you have probable cause."

"Do I?" Jax turned toward me. "One of the prime suspects, who I must admit is being very sneaky herself, just told me that a mysterious will was signed *conveniently* the day before the victim died. And it left a bunch of money to his wife, who is also a suspect. How do I know who to believe?"

"Jax...come on. You know me! I wouldn't lie..."

"What if your source lied? I don't even know who your source is."

"Father Olaf, you guessed it..."

"I thought you didn't want me to pass that information along, so I *forgot* about it like you asked."

I looked down, at a loss for words. "What do you want me to say?"

"Nothing. Let's go get you a phone. I have my guys looking into this. If there was a will signed in this town, we'll find out about it. Very soon. Probably by the time we're done getting your phone."

I sighed.

"Don't worry. We've got men watching her on a regular basis anyway."

"Do you have them on all the suspects?" I asked. I stepped back and gasped. "*You're* watching me, you sneak."

"You asked me to come with, if you'll remember. I don't know what you're talking about."

"You little *sneak*."

"Listen, you asked me to help you out. I'd be just as happy back in my office."

"Okay, then please feel free to go back to your office. I'm more than happy to take care of this myself." I put my hand on the knob of the front door and twisted hard. I wasn't sure what I was expecting to happen. Mostly I wanted to relieve some anger. But instead, the knob came off right in my hand, and the door swung wide open.

"Whoops," I said, glancing down at the knob now dangling between my fingers.

Jax's features scrunched up in exasperation, as if he didn't want to believe what he was seeing.

"Looks like I've been invited in." I stepped into the sorry excuse for a home, immediately plugging my nose. "Smells like something died in here."

I felt Jax freeze behind me. I hadn't realized he'd been so close to me, but his hand clasped my arm and his muscles tightened on the word *died*.

"Poor choice of words," I said. "It just smells terrible. But it could be because of *that*." I pointed to a molding pile of garbage in what used to be the garbage can but now looked more like a compost pile.

"I don't think she's been here recently," Jax said.

"She was at class."

"Have you seen her since?"

I paused, taking in the violently gross kitchen. The tequila bottle and citrus peels were where we'd left them after our first visit. "I don't think she's a great housekeeper. She could just be tolerating this smell."

"Nobody can tolerate this smell."

I nodded. Speaking of, the smell was getting to me. I leaned a hand against the counter. "Okay, you're right. It's making me nauseous."

"Let's do a quick scan of the place. Make sure she didn't OD in her bathtub or something." Jax strode past me without so much as flinching at the smell. Apparently he'd seen some nasty things on the job and had learned to put up with it. Either that or he was born with one of the strongest stomachs I'd ever encountered.

Jax must have noticed my struggle to stand upright. He extended his arm, and I grasped it like an inner tube that'd been tossed to save me in the middle of a particularly stormy ocean. I hung on for dear life, choking back gags as we started through the house.

There was nothing and nobody in the dilapidated bathroom, nothing and nobody in the living room or the hallways. All that was left in the tiny place was the bedroom.

"Ooh," I gasped. "This isn't good." At the sight before us, I turned around and waited out the waves of nausea in the hallway as Jax rubbed my back lightly.

Once I was under control, he took out his phone and placed a call.

"We need some guys over here, stat. Potential murder scene."

Jax did a quick scan of the room after hanging up the phone. He looked back at me. "We've got one hitch. I don't see a body."

Whether or not it was a murder scene, we couldn't be certain until there was a body. What I was certain of was that there had been some sort of struggle based on the amount of blood on the bed, the carpet, and even the wall.

"There's a good amount of blood," Jax said. "Whoever's it is doesn't have a great chance of surviving."

"What is that?" I asked. Jax hadn't let me enter the room any further, mostly so I didn't destroy a potential crime scene if my stomach revolted on me, but I peeked around the doorframe regardless.

One of the pillows was stabbed all the way through with a long, ugly knife. It looked suspiciously like the one wielded by Mrs. Jenkins the night Donna and I had stopped by. *Had we barely escaped with our lives that night?* The thought turned my stomach. *What was I doing putting a mother of five children in danger?*

"Our killer has left us a note, it appears," Jax said.

He gingerly leaned across the bed without touching anything and read the note aloud.

"My dear Anthony. When will you leave your wife? My heart is breaking. I can't bear to spend my evenings with you, only to go home alone. I'll give you one week, and then it's over. I'll never stop loving you, but I need to stop torturing myself. With love..."

Jax turned toward me.

"With love from who?" I asked.

"The note is ripped below the name," he said with downturned lips.

"Mrs. Jenkins probably wanted us to work for the name of the victim," I guessed. "If we don't know who it is, we don't even know whose body to look *for.*"

"How do you think she got Anthony's lover to come here, into her home? If it is Anthony's mistress's blood."

"Force?" I shrugged. "Or maybe the girl found out about the will and came here to confront Mrs. Jenkins. Maybe she wanted the money. There's a bunch of reasons."

Jax nodded. "There's nothing more you can do here, Misty. Listen, I have a bunch of guys on the way. Take my car and go get a phone. We can't have you hanging around the crime scene anyway. I'll get a ride back to the station, and you can drive my car to your place. I've got the squad car I can use."

Jax handed over a key.

"That's...thank you," I said. "I'd like to stay though."

"We won't find out anything for a while, and I'll call you when I do. The team won't be happy if you're mucking up the scene when they get here. Speaking of...I think I hear them now. Give your statement and go. I'll have a patrol car follow you to the phone store at least until we find Mrs. Jenkins. If this is a crime of passion like I think it might be, then you're probably out of the woods. But it's better to be safe than sorry. Especially until we find her."

I backed away, horrified, but too intrigued to rip my eyes from the scene. Finally, the smell overwhelmed me, and I headed outside, giving my statement to a friendly cop who thankfully wasn't Alfie.

Once I finished, I took the keys and hopped into Jax's car, cruising away. Jax had mentioned that I should let the cops know when I took off, but I was only going to the phone store. That was a public, safe place. I'd give Jax a call from my new phone and tell him when I was headed home. He'd be proud that I kept him updated *and* got a new phone. Double score.

On the way to the store though, I had a sudden ping of guilt. The woman who'd been in love with Anthony—she'd been wrong to sleep with a married man, yes. But did she deserve to be brutally murdered for it?

I took a brief detour. The comic store was supposedly closed today, but I had a gut feeling that the store was never *completely* closed. Maybe a member would be there to let me in. If I could just locate someone who had a better idea of who this girl was, maybe we could find her body. Her family deserved to know, if nothing else.

I whipped Jax's car into a parking space out front. I wasn't really worried about anyone seeing it. I'd only be inside for a few short seconds. Walking up to the door with a million different knobs, I realized I still wasn't quite sure how to get inside the joint.

First, I tried the same handle that'd caused the door to swing open before. Nothing, except the small electric jolt I'd gotten the first time. But this time, there was no swinging door that accompanied it.

I tried another one that set off a rooster-like sound inside the building, and then the next, which was incredibly slippery and made my hand feel like it'd bathed in olive oil, and the last, which was unpleasantly slimy.

"Come on," I said. "Open sesame."

I kicked the door, and this time it swung open a bit.

Wow, I thought. I was two for two at this whole *getting locked doors opened* thing today.

But this time, a face awaited me on the other side of the door.

"Merlin?" I asked.

Father Olaf was dressed in his purple cloak once more, looking both resigned and extraordinarily tired. "What is it?"

"I...I need to ask a favor."

"Haven't you already asked enough?"

"Actually, just about," I said. "But there's one more thing...and this time it's not for me."

"What is it then?"

"The girl—I *really* need to know who she is. The one Anthony liked."

"I told you, nobody knows her name. Not her real name."

"Bullshit," I retorted. Then I remembered that I was talking not only to Merlin but also to a priest. "Sorry. Bull-crapola. Somebody better know something because there's a *very* good chance this girl is dead."

Merlin gasped. "Dead? No. She can't be. Alfie said she might be coming by tonight..."

I gave Merlin the evil eye.

"I was going to call you," he hedged.

"Well, I just came from a pretty gnarly crime scene, and unless Anthony had more than one lover, things don't look good for her."

"That's…that's terrible."

"Yes, it is. But we don't have her body. We need a body, or else there's no crime. And a body might just lead us to Mrs. Jenkins. This is about more than some comic stuff, or whatever, that you guys are into. This is about life and death. Help me, please."

"Come in. We can talk more inside."

I followed the swirly purple cape into the comic store. The dark passageway melded into a room full of books, which was a blur. It wasn't until we'd reached the simple desk in the middle of the room that he stopped.

"What do you need from me?" he asked. "I assume the information will be kept in the greatest confidence."

"Yeah, yes. How can you even worry about that right now? A girl's life is at stake." I looked at Merlin. "We need to find her, in case there's a chance she's still alive."

The priest's eyes blinked once, a heaviness to his eyelids. "I don't know who…"

"You've *got* to know. Don't you guys have some inkling of who she might be? This town isn't exactly huge in size. In fact, it's not even a city. This girl can't have been coming from *that* far away. Someone had to know her." I took a step closer to Merlin. "Who was she?"

"There's one thing that might help," he started.

"Well? We don't have time to waste."

"Follow me then." Merlin took a step further to the back of the room, but a crash from the other direction stalled him where he stood.

"Let's go," I said. "Hurry."

Merlin raised a finger and pointed behind me.

I wheeled around, my throat constricting with shock and fear.

"We found the other half of the note." Jax spoke first, his large figure taking up most of the doorway. His face was stony, and I had the feeling I knew what he had come to tell me.

"With love from *who*?" I whispered. My heart sank to the very pit of my stomach below my navel, and chills took hold of my veins.

"With love, from *Misty*." Jax dropped his gaze. "If that blood in there is from Mrs. Jenkins, things do *not* look great for you, Misty."

I sank to my knees. "No. No, no, no. It wasn't—I never wrote a note! How could it have been me?"

I swiveled on my knees, feeling the urge to vomit once more. But nothing came up this time, as my stomach was completely, brutally empty.

"I've got to arrest you, Misty," Jax said without apology. "For the murder of Anthony Jenkins."

"No. No, you've got to believe me. Why would I have tried so hard to get into her house if I'd left the note? With you right there. That makes no sense. Come on, Jax."

"Misty—I've got a probable murder weapon stabbing a note with your name on it. Not to mention, you were the one who suggested it was Mrs. Jenkins doing the killing and not the other way around. It didn't dawn on me that Mrs. Jenkins might be the victim of a scorned lover, not right away at least, thanks to your *suggestion*."

"Jax, check the blood, check for fingerprints. Even if it looks bad, it wasn't me. I was framed," I said, using lingo I'd heard on TV. I wasn't a cop. I wasn't a killer. I was just trying to run a small business.

Jax looked resigned. "I'm going to get everything checked out, and if it wasn't you, then you can be sure we'll get to the bottom of it, and we'll release you. But fingerprints, blood work, it takes some time. I'm sorry. You're under arrest."

Jax snapped handcuffs around me.

I didn't even resist. I felt so weak. But another thought was puzzling me just as much. If Mrs. Jenkins wasn't the killer— where was she?

CHAPTER SIXTEEN

———

Things could've been worse. Though, they weren't particularly pretty. I was in a private cell, thankfully, locked away in the sleepy town's sleepy jail. A cop I'd gone to high school with sat out front munching on some Doritos, and I was so hungry I was tempted to lick the orange dust from his fingertips.

"Can I get a coffee?" I asked. "Froot Loops? Anything, please."

The cop ignored me. I wasn't sure what his current strategy was. The police had initially fed me and chatted freely, probing for information and asking me for a confession. I didn't give them one. I eventually realized that I would go nowhere, including a jail cell, until I lawyered up or gave them a confession. I chose to ask for a lawyer.

My call had been to Donna, asking for her help once again. I really needed to buy her a nice large steak once this was all over. Or maybe a cake. Or a lot of wine so we could be happy and forget everything that had happened. Money might not buy happiness, but it bought bubbly, which gave me quite a bit of happiness. That was, if I ever got out of this cell.

"Is anyone coming to help me?" I was beginning to sound whiney, but I didn't know what else to do. I couldn't afford a fancy-pants lawyer, I didn't know anyone who could, and I was *still* locked up for a crime I had nothing to do with.

"What did Donna say?" My high school acquaintance chewed on his lip.

"She reamed Jax out when she heard he arrested me, but he didn't change his mind."

"Then I ain't changing my mind," he said. "Jax is the boss around here."

"But you have the power to help me," I begged.

"And I'm gonna use that power to enjoy my Doritos, here." He flicked the paper up and read some more.

I lay back on my small little cot, kneading my hands against my forehead.

Eventually, his eyes flicked over to me. "Say, whatever happened to you after high school? You kinda up and left. We all thought you was a nerd and went to get real smart at college."

"Yeah, yeah. Didn't work, did it?" I snapped.

"Hey, Misty. I'm just trying to chat with you. I get paid to sit here, and I can make things miserable or actually quite pleasant."

I sighed. "Sorry. It's just…my nerves are shot. I'm extremely tired. I've barely had enough to eat, and I'm framed for a crime I didn't commit."

"Sucks, man. Dorito?" he meandered over and held the bag out for me.

"Thanks." I took a few, crunching them with what was probably a sour expression on my face. Not because of the Doritos. Those were, in fact, quite tasty.

"Tell me your story. Maybe I'll take sympathy on you."

"Will you really?"

"Nah, I need the job. Got three kids at home, and they're gonna have to go to college someday, I suppose. But talking to you is better'n reading the paper. Plus, you'll be in the paper tomorrow anyway. I might as well get a jump start on the news. The missus will love a jump on the gossip. Er—news."

I rolled my eyes. But misery loves company, and I started the whole story. The whole sob story about moving to LA after college to obtain a fancy degree with lots of letters I could marry to my name. But in doing so, how I'd ended up with a broken heart and a surprising gig I loved, dancing at the burlesque clubs around the city. I finished the story in one giant circle, ending with how I'd arrived back here, splat in the middle of Little Lake's six-celled jail.

"Why did you stop dancing?" he asked. I really needed to learn his name. But by this point, it had turned into one of those moments where I'd let conversation go on for far too long before asking him to tell me his name again. The cop had both feet on the desk, a hand behind his head, and the other tipping the bag of Doritos straight into his mouth so he could drink the crumbs.

"Hello, *monsieur*." Donna strolled into the room looking very put together and dashing in tight jeans and a low-scooped top, an edgy little leather jacket completing the look.

The cop kicked his feet off the desk. "What can I do for you? Here to see Jax?"

"Yes, actually. Is he in?" Donna purred.

"I think he might've headed for home, as a matter of fact..." The cop glanced behind him. Jax's office wasn't far away, and I could almost read my high school buddy's face as he debated how embarrassing it would be if he called Jax on the phone versus walked the two doors down to get him.

"Would you mind checking? I would, but I don't want to barge in on him," Donna said.

"Not at all. I'll check now. Can I grab you coffee on the way?"

"Sure, I'd love some decaf. Actually, let's be honest. I'd *love* me some regular coffee, but I'm breastfeeding and all, the babies..." Donna said with a roll of her eye.

I stared at Donna. There was no way Donna was breastfeeding her youngest. But she must have a reason for leading the front desk attendant on to believe it. *What was she up to?*

I watched silently, playing along, hoping I'd catch on to whatever Donna was aiming to achieve. As she leaned toward my unnamed high school buddy and slipped her jacket off, real slowly down one arm, her tactic suddenly dawned on me. The cop froze with a Dorito halfway to his mouth, and I didn't think the drool was for the chip.

I nearly rolled my eyes, but then it hit me. The guy's name was Dwight. He'd *always* had a crush on Donna. He'd asked her to prom every year in school and been rejected every time. Talk about unrequited love.

"Let me take your jacket for you," Dwight insisted.

"Thanks, but that's all right." Donna's eyes flicked toward me as she kept a firm hold of her jacket.

"No, really. Let me hang it up," Dwight insisted.

"I'll only be a second, honest," Donna said.

"No, no." Dwight more forcefully pulled the jacket from her, simultaneously putting his hand on her shoulder. "You asked for a cup o' Joe, and I'm gonna bring you the best cup you've had this year. You sit down and sip it, Donna. I insist. You work yourself too hard."

Donna's smile was frozen on her face as he pulled the jacket away.

"Everything all right?" Dwight asked.

"Yep." Donna blushed. "Well, as a matter of fact, I have a *teensy* favor to ask of you."

"Name it." Dwight was back leaning on the desk lickety-split.

"I need to...tinkle, and if you don't mind, I'd *really* like to use the private one." She grinned. "But I'm not sure I can wait to grab Jax's key—do you think I could use yours?"

Dwight pulled out a jingling set of keys from his pocket. He looked incredibly torn at the moment—I could almost read his mind. Now was his chance to do a favor for the girl he'd had his eye on for years. Of course, now they were both happily married, but there was something about young love that was hard to let go. On the other hand, the private bathroom keys were strapped to the rest of his keys, and handing that stash over surely went against protocol.

Dwight's eyes shifted down the hallway, glancing toward Jax's office. "Can you wait one second?"

"Oh, no. No, I can't, but that's okay. I'll just use the public one. The same one *she* uses." Donna tilted her chin at me, her voice insinuating I was the scum of the earth. "It's my special time. I can't *exactly* wait. It's a little...out of my control."

Dwight shoved the keys out to Donna and dashed down the hall like his pants were disappearing in flames.

"Your special time?" I glanced at Donna. "Beautiful. Really, poetic."

She rushed over, jangling the keys, trying the first one in the lock. "Yeah, yeah. Old Dwight. What a nerd."

But from her downcast eyes and pink-tinged cheek, she was completely transparent.

I grinned. "You *like* Dwight having a crush on you."

"You try having five kids. It does a number on your self-esteem." She turned her hand, and the lock clicked open.

"You are gorgeous," I said. "You look like you're twenty-two. And act like it too. Thanks for busting me out, girlfriend."

"Anytime." Her eyes gleamed. "Crap. My phone is in that jacket though, the one with Dwight."

"We don't have time." The coffeepot dripped in the background, and Dwight whistled extra loudly, probably trying to block out sounds of any girl stuff that might be happening.

"But what if the kids call? Alec has been finicky, and I think he might be coming down with something..." Donna said.

"Nathan has a phone," I said. "He's a good dad. And I'll bring you straight home. Let's *go*."

Donna cast one glance down the hall. "He'll kill me."

"Dwight or Nathan?" I asked, glancing after her.

Donna just glared at me.

"Don't worry. Jax will probably kill me first." I grabbed her hand and yanked her out of her reverie as I heard the smack of a fridge door sealing shut and the clatter of a coffee cup being set on a plate.

Together we rushed out and hopped into her car, Donna in the driver's seat and me in the passenger seat.

She wheeled out of the parking lot, and we were two blocks away before Dwight rushed out looking wildly up and down the street. I squinted, barely able to make out his figure as Donna drove us out of sight.

"I don't think he saw us," I said as Donna whipped down a narrow alley. She knew this town better than the back of her hand.

"He won't chase us," Donna said. "He'll go tell Nathan. He'll probably wet his pants doing so, but...ah well. Poor guy."

"I still think you have a soft spot for him. Just a teensy bit," I said. "Innocent crush?"

"Shut up." Donna stared straight ahead. "Tell me, how were you gonna bring me straight home anyway? Did you steal a car? Don't tell me that's why I got a call from you in prison."

"I didn't steal a car. But I would've offered to drive *yours*. Anyway, the situation's complicated."

"Please, fill me in."

I gave Donna the nitty-gritty details. All the while, she made hairpin turns, backtracked, and rattled down side streets as if driving a getaway car was her nighttime gig.

When I finished, she let out a low whistle. "Things don't look great for you, do they?"

I shook my head, glancing at her. "You still think I didn't do it, right?"

"Of course not. I've got kids in this town. I wouldn't have broken a killer out of jail. In fact, I consider busting you out my good deed of the day," she said with a light smile.

"How so?"

"Because you need to figure out who put you in this mess so we can get the real killer off the streets. Like I said, I got kids in this town. I want it to be a safe place."

I nodded. "I really appreciate this. I was thinking in jail—"

"Don't tell me you suddenly found your savior or something—you were in there five minutes."

"Actually, I was thinking I should buy you a nice steak and some bubbly after this to celebrate."

"Make it two bottles," Donna said. "I'm not gonna be getting any action from Nathan anytime soon after pulling this stunt, so I might need something else to help me sleep."

I grinned, and it felt good. I hadn't had a lot to smile about the past few days. "Drive yourself home. If I can ask one last favor, would you mind dropping me off at the comic book store?"

"I've got until three this afternoon, when I have to head to school for the science fair. Nathan Jr.'s volcano is going to explode at three fifteen on the dot, and if I don't take a video, he'll *flip*."

"Thanks. Just drop me, and head home. I don't want you involved in this anymore."

Donna parked a few blocks away in a dirty little alley I'd never been in before. Which was impressive, considering I thought I knew every inch of this tiny town.

"Wow, I didn't know this was here," I said, climbing out of the car. We were blocks away from the comic store. It was a brilliant park job. Nobody would ever find it. Unless... "Does Nathan know about this place?"

Donna smiled smugly. "I made out with Angelo D'Amico back here when I was thirteen. First time a boy touched my boob."

I remembered—he was the teenage bad boy who'd broken most girls' hearts at Little Lake high.

Donna sighed wistfully in remembrance. "I could never bring Nathan here...he'd be too jealous."

I wrinkled my nose, not sure if Nathan would be jealous of a boob graze in seventh grade, but then again, Angelo D'Amico had been good lookin'. "Where did Angelo end up?"

"Driving a FedEx truck. Ugly dude these days, but back then..." She shook her head. "Smokin'."

We crept up to the back of the comic book shop. It was supposedly closed today, but there was no difference in signage from any other day.

"What's our plan?" Donna hissed.

"I have a theory," I said. "Someone knows information in here, but I don't know who. I figure if I can find a way to *convince* them to tell me..."

"You're threatening the priest again. Lord have mercy." Donna made the sign of the cross.

"No." I winced. "Maybe I'll threaten Alfie."

"Oh, good. The cop." Donna made praying hands and mumbled something.

"It's for a good cause."

"To find the killer."

"Exactly. Except, Alfie's working, so he's safe, for the moment."

"What are you going to threaten them with?" she asked.

"I don't know." I knocked.

The door swung open, and I faced a black hole once again.

"Is anyone there?" I asked.

There was no response.

I shrugged at Donna, then took the first step forward. It was my neck on the line. I wasn't trying to be brave. In fact, I was shaking so hard my hand couldn't have dialed 9-1-1 if I tried.

"Hello?" We crept to the right, back to where we'd been standing the other night when Merlin revealed himself. There was a book sitting out on the table, a dusting brush next to it, as if someone had been cleaning it before we'd arrived.

The book was a huge one, so I grabbed it with both hands, just in case. It wasn't like I had a gun on me. Or a Taser. Or even pepper spray. They'd even taken my nail clippers at the jailhouse. I had to be resourceful.

"There." Donna nodded toward the hallway from which Father Olaf and Alfie had emerged the other night.

Except today, the two candles on either side of the doorway were lit. They flickered, casting an eerie glow around the dim room, the light dancing dangerously over the comic book covers.

I nodded moving forward, feeling like I was getting closer and closer to a sleeping bear's lair. And I doubted the consequences would be good. But there was no other way. I was now a fugitive, and I not only needed answers, I needed them *fast*.

No sooner had I taken the first step through the doorway than a rustle sounded behind me. Both Donna and I whirled around.

"Sorry," I mumbled, after a near miss of Donna's head with the heavy book I wielded in my hands.

Father Olaf stood behind us, his arms spread open. "To what do I owe this visit?"

"I need answers," I said.

Father Olaf raised one hand to his head, and I saw he held a cell phone. "9-1-1 is already dialed. I'm pressing the button, and you will be caught. You are now a fugitive, and I'm no longer afraid of you. My secret is out."

An iciness crept down the vertebrae in my back. I didn't think Father Olaf would hurt us, but he had nothing to lose anymore. Or nothing to gain by helping us out, at least.

I lifted the book a bit higher, and Father Olaf winced.

I glanced at Donna, who looked shocked. It wasn't like I was actually going to *hit* the priest. I was just shifting. The book was heavy.

"Uh, Misty?" Donna pointed behind me.

The very edge of the book had accidentally grazed the tip of the flame when I'd lifted it higher. The corner was very slightly singed, like a marshmallow just starting to brown.

"Aha," I said, the idea popping into my head. "You like this book?"

"Please." Merlin reached his hands out. "It's one of a kind. There's none like it."

"Probably why you were giving it a special cleaning." I raised an eyebrow.

He looked down. "Please, it's priceless."

"Yeah, well, so is my life, and I don't intend to spend it in jail." I looked at him seriously. "I'm not kidding. I have nothing to lose. I am extremely sorry to do this to you, but I need answers. I need a name. I need a number. If I don't get one of those in the next thirty seconds, this book is turning back into ashes."

"I don't have any information," Merlin said. "Honest, I don't know—"

I lifted the book closer toward the flame, and the corner started to melt just a bit.

Merlin whimpered.

"Stop lying," I said. "It's against the Commandments."

"Fine! Check the computer."

"Where's the computer?" I asked. "You just thought to tell me about the computer *now*?"

"It's in the room behind you," he said.

"No luck. I'm not falling for that. I'm staying right here, keeping this book nice and toasty by the flames," I said. I really hoped he'd get a move on with the information. My biceps were built for dancing, not for holding boulders above my head for ages. "You have internet on your phone, don't you?"

Merlin waited forever to respond. My arms were wobbly, and I was about to break down and follow him into the next room without a plan. I was getting desperate, and my arms were getting tired. However, just before my arms collapsed, I saw a crack in his resolve. "Yes."

"Tell me," I roared, the pain really getting to me now. It was like trying to hold on to the monkey bars for a year.

"I know her first name. I only know this because I poked around after you were arrested because I was curious. I can't find her last name, honest. But I have her address. It's real. A few weeks ago, there was an accounting mix up, and we didn't have enough cash on hand to pay the girls. Anthony knew where she lived, and I found a note stuck in his things."

"How do I know it's real? What if it's the address to Anthony's grandmother's house?" I asked.

"I drove by the address myself today. It's her—no doubt about it. I recognized the walk. The hair."

"Here's what we're gonna do. You're gonna give me the slip of paper with her name and address on it. You give us a fifteen-minute head start, then call the cops or don't. I'm taking the book with me. If the information is good, the book will be returned."

The priest nodded, his face resigned.

"We have a deal?" I pressed.

"Yes." He reached his hand out, and we shook on it. When I withdrew my hand, it was holding a piece of paper.

I glanced down at it, my mouth feeling like it'd come unhinged. All the saliva dried at the writing on the paper. "No."

The priest nodded.

"No," I said again.

Donna reached over and grabbed the paper from my outstretched hand. I was as frozen as a gargoyle in shock.

"No," Donna said. "No."

The priest nodded. "If you leave the book, I won't call the cops on you ladies."

I dropped the book on the table, rather unceremoniously, and hurried out of the shop with Donna close at my heels.

Unfortunately, we both knew the address to where we were headed, as well as the name on the paper.

CHAPTER SEVENTEEN

———

"I should've known." I shook my head.

Crouching next to Donna behind a fluffy bush, we hid directly across the street from the house in question. We'd parked a few blocks away and walked to the address listed on the slip of paper, so as not to arouse suspicion.

The house was small and modest, an easy-to-afford starter home for the single woman. The yard was boxy and simple. The place would look decent with minimal amounts of lawn care, and there wasn't much of a walkway that would need shoveling in the coldest months of winter. The few bushes out front sprouted dusty leaves, which rattled with the chill in the air.

"How? You were trying to be a good person. Heck, nobody guessed. Not even Jax," Donna said.

I gave Donna a small smile, but my attention was drawn back to the house as a cop car rolled to a stop out front. Squinting, I could make out Jax in the driver's seat, his girlfriend sitting next to him.

"Trouble in paradise?" Donna asked as we watched what looked like an animated argument take place. "He doesn't look happy."

Even I couldn't feel happy about this latest development, however, because Jax was sitting across the seat from Sarah, whose address was on the slip of paper that Father Olaf handed over to me. The chances were high that he was staring into the eyes of a murderer. Or now, kissing a murderer.

"Wow, that was fast," I said, glancing away as the animated conversation turned from a discussion into a steamy good-bye kiss. I wondered what had spurred Sarah to need a ride home, when I knew she had her own car.

"It's over. You can look now," Donna said, removing the hand she'd clasped over my eyes as the two locked lips. "Plus, she's getting out, which isn't a good sign for them. I think she's been staying at his place a lot, so maybe they need some time apart to cool off."

"We should signal Jax. I'm not sure it's a great idea to go after her by ourselves."

"Go after her? Nope, I wasn't planning on doing that. She's got crazy eyes," Donna said, shaking her head.

"She does, doesn't she?" A wave of relief washed over me. "I thought I was just biased from a stupid kindergarten grudge, but I couldn't get over the fact that she has crazy eyes."

"Nuts."

"Psycho."

I glanced at my friend and smiled. "Thanks."

"What sort of a friend would let you face a psycho on her own?"

"You?" I asked. "I think I'm going to go in there. I am an escaped convict. I don't have much time. In fact, Jax wouldn't probably even believe me if I signaled him now."

"That's not a smart plan. The woman has killed at least one person, who she supposedly *loved*, and possibly another. I don't like the odds of her letting you waltz out of there unscathed," Donna said.

"What about your faith in me?" I flexed my smallish arms, trying to lighten the mood with a grin.

Donna shook her head. "Those mashed potatoes aren't getting you anywhere. And, girl, you can dance like none other, but I'm afraid those skills aren't going to help you here either, unless you plan on seducing her."

"Not a bad idea." I raised an eyebrow.

"I'm not letting you go in there."

"Come on. It's the only chance I've got. I'll go back to jail if we call the cops, and there's a chance Sarah will never be caught."

"They'll look into it. The cops will figure out who did it, and if it's Sarah, they'll arrest her."

"But they'll be looking closest at me—especially since I broke out of jail. You're not *totally* innocent in this either, missy."

"Actually, that's a good point. I'm surprised I haven't heard from Nathan yet, asking where I went…" Her eyes got large as she looked up at me. "I don't have a phone. And neither do you, I'm assuming."

I gave a queasy smile. "Nope."

"Excellent."

"At least they can't track us," I said with a halfhearted smile.

"I kind of want someone tracking us. Especially if we're talking about going into the house of a *murderer*."

I looked at Donna. "We can't get the cops involved yet. They'll be too concerned about asking us *stuff*, and we don't have a ton of evidence on Sarah. Especially not stuff that can be explained quick and easy…"

"And without giving away Alfie. Jax knows about Father Olaf."

"Exactly." I looked up. "Plus, the more time we waste, the greater the chances are that we don't find Mrs. Jenkins alive. And I don't think she killed her husband."

Donna's face turned stony. "But I don't want to lose you too. If Mrs. Jenkins is already dead, I'm not letting you risk your life."

"But I don't want to spend my life behind bars."

"I won't let that happen. There's no evidence on you."

"Except for my fishnets at the crime scene!"

"I'll break you out again if I have to."

Donna and I were locked into a staring contest, both of us breathing heavy, neither of us ready to relent.

"Here's the deal," I said. "I don't want to lose Sarah. It's unlikely, but what if Father Olaf or Alfie got in touch with her and told her we're onto her? Or maybe Jax mentioned that I was broken out of jail—if he knows about it, which he probably does. Either way, she might be getting ready to run. I would, if I were her."

"And your idea to stop her is…"

"I think you should go to the cops. We don't have a phone, but the station's not far. Take the car. Go talk to Nathan or Jax. They'll believe you much more than they'll believe me," I said.

"What do you want me to tell them?"

"Tell them exactly what's been happening, what we found out, what Father Olaf told us. Get Alfie to back you up if you need—after all we've tried to do for him, we can only hope he'll help us. Gauge if they believe you. But go straight to Jax and Nathan. I still don't know who broke into my house and used a cop car to get away, so we can't take any chances of someone on the force hearing about this if they're in cahoots with Sarah."

"Of course."

"If they seem ready to work with you after all that, tell them you'll bring them to me *only* if they promise to arrest Sarah as well. They can take me in if they want, but I'm not going without her," I said.

Donna nodded. "What will you be doing?"

"I'm going to stay here. Keep an eye on the house."

"And if she leaves?"

"I don't have a car. How could I follow her?" I shrugged. "If she leaves, the best I can do is pay attention to which way she goes and wait for you to come back."

"You won't go in after her by yourself?"

"No." I wanted to cross my fingers behind my back, but I owed this much to Donna. "I promise you. I'll wait. I have faith you can convince Nathan or Jax. But you have to go now, and you have to hurry. Jax won't like to hear that his girlfriend is…uh, not who he expected."

Donna nodded. "Don't do anything dangerous."

I gave her a one-armed hug, and she kissed my cheek. "You got it. I plan to buy you a big steak after this, and I plan to be alive, eating one with you."

Donna hustled away, ducking into the shrubbery until she was in the clear on the other side of the block. I watched as she got into the car and cruised away, off to convince the cops to let me be free.

I hunkered down behind the bushes and settled in to wait. For the first few minutes, I tried to get comfortable amid the branches poking me in the ear and the leaves scratching against my neck. When a huge spider crawled on the stick directly in front of my face, I leapt backward, stumbling through the bushes.

The leaves rustled and the branches shook. Despite the loudness, I couldn't do anything about it. It was a huge spider. And I really didn't like spiders. I crouched behind the bush, a safe distance back, but I couldn't see much from across the street. Maybe if I took a few steps closer...

Slipping across the street was easier than I expected. There'd been no sign of Sarah so far. Not even a shadow in the window. It was a little worrying since the house was small, and I could see through the window panel by the front door all the way through to the backyard.

But she could be in the small upper level or the garage that peeked out from behind the house. It was a good sign she wasn't watching through her front windows, or I'd surely have been discovered by my tumble through the underbrush.

A large evergreen sat watch next to her front window, and now that I was on her side of the street, I could see a small opening under the branches, the perfect-sized burrow for a human around my height. If I could just sneak past the front windows...

A few seconds later I'd zipped across the front yard, after a few minutes of careful scanning of the surroundings. But the neighborhood appeared quiet, the houses spread out and independent. Some had hedges, others fences, and still others had landscaping that encouraged private yards and minding one's own business.

It was easy to sneak under the wide, outstretched arms of the Christmas-style tree, and I even found my new habitat to be warm and comfortable. It would be simple to wait here until Donna came back, cops in tow.

The dried, crispy brown tree needles created a nifty little blanket for me to kneel on, while the fullness of the branches covered me almost completely. I could see all of the yard, including the front door and a generous peek into the living room window. I hadn't seen any movement in the house yet, but there was no way Sarah could've left. From my hiding spot, I could see straight through the living room back to the garage, which was silent and dark.

My lack of phone was slightly irritating when I realized I couldn't check how long had passed since Donna had left and I'd migrated to my new hiding spot. Maybe it'd been one minute, and Donna wasn't even to the station yet. Or maybe it'd been thirty minutes, and Donna was already back, promising to show the cops my hiding place and discovering I'd jumped ship.

Dang, I thought. Maybe I should've left a note, or an arrow made out of sticks, or *something* to show the direction I'd headed. I glanced back at the house. All was still motionless. Maybe I could scoot back across the lawn really quickly, check if Donna was parked down the street, and leave a small note...

A mumbled voice drew my attention back to the house. It was coming from the upstairs, I suspected. From the outside, there appeared to be a small, itty-bitty loft above the living room. Certainly not enough space for a bedroom, but maybe enough space for storage. Storage of what, I was hesitant to find out.

The curtain in the window of the upper level billowed lightly, and I thought I could make out a shadow inside the room. Unless it was a breeze from the outside and my eyes were playing tricks on me, which was entirely possible. All this waiting was starting to mess with my head, the smallest noises causing me to flinch.

But wait—the window was *shut*. The motion wasn't due to a breeze. There was someone up there.

I scooted back, very slowly. I had to get closer. I had to see if that was Mrs. Jenkins up there.

But as I scooted back, I bumped my head on something that hadn't been there moments before. My spine tingled, and my gut clenched as the cool metal of what may or may not have been a gun pressed to the back of my head.

A very calm, very collected voice spoke. "You're going to want to stand up *very* slowly and come with me."

I stood up, arms raised, and very slowly turned to face my archenemy from kindergarten. Her blue eyes, which I'd dismissed as cute and quirky, were now icy.

They were crazy eyes, for sure, but not crazy in the sense of a psychotic mental patient. They were crazy because they were so calm, so wide, and so determined. I had little doubt she'd shoot me in a second, and even less she wouldn't think twice about doing it.

"Sarah, it doesn't have to be like this," I said. "Please, I just wanted to see..."

"What did you want to see?" Sarah gave a chuckle, though her face was covered in a grimace. "Me kiss the *love of your life*? Me finish off Mrs. Jenkins? Me rock some sexy burlesque moves for your man-crush?"

"Is Mrs. Jenkins alive? Please, let her go. We can talk."

"She's alive, but not for long. Plus, it's too late to help her anyway. Or it will be too late by the time people find her." She shrugged.

"Where is she?" I had to keep her talking. It was my only chance. I was unarmed, with only a few pine needles and maybe a dry stick or two at my disposal. Meanwhile, Sarah had a gun on her, which she obviously wasn't afraid to use.

If I could keep her talking outside the house, Donna was bound to come back sooner or later, hopefully with the police. I needed to get a confession from Sarah. But too early, and nobody would hear it, and it'd probably leave me dead before the others arrived. Too late, and Mrs. Jenkins would die.

Sarah shrugged. "Doesn't matter. She was old anyway."

"But she didn't deserve to *die*. And neither did her husband."

Sarah barked a laugh. "What do you know about Anthony?"

"Not a whole lot, which is why I am *clueless* as to why you pinned his murder on me," I said, pushing a stray hair back from my face.

"It was too easy. Much too easy, Misty. Plus, you always hated me. I needed someone to blame, and you were it. Really, don't take it too personally."

"You've always been psycho! Ever since kindergarten," I said, unable to keep the bitterness out of my voice.

"And you've always been pretty and smart and successful. How about leaving the rest of us something to do well at?" Sarah retorted.

"What?" I gaped at her. "You're *jealous* of me?"

"Not anymore, ironically. Which was an unplanned bonus of this whole debacle. Enough talk. I don't want to kill you out here. People might hear. Walk back toward the garage, and if you move a muscle, I'll shoot."

I scanned the path for anything I could use against Sarah. A stick, a spare shovel, a leftover ball from a neighbor kid. But there was nothing. Her yard was immaculate. Almost as if she was prepared for the situation.

"Press the button," she said, gesturing next to the garage door. "The big one. Anything funny, you move a muscle, and you're dead."

I pressed the button. Sarah stayed just far enough behind me so that I couldn't lash out at her with a foot or swing an elbow. She was good. She was careful. She was calculating. And she didn't seem to be taking any stupid risks, which was probably how she'd gotten this far without getting caught in the first place.

My stomach jolted a few notches. I didn't have a good feeling about how this would end. As the garage door opened, I wasn't sure what to expect. *Dead bodies? Mrs. Jenkins?* Though I hadn't known what to expect, I'd expected *something.* Not the barren room before me. There was nothing in the garage. Not a car, not a shelf—nothing. With the exception of a suitcase and a small purse in the corner, the place was spotless and empty.

"Going somewhere?" I asked.

"Might take a sunny vacation for a bit when all this is over. I really can't stand any more of Jax's *nagging.* Commitment this, commitment that...but then again, you and I—we have that in common, don't we?" She smiled. "You ran away from him too. Poor Jax. Will the guy ever learn?"

She crooked an eyebrow, which served to turn some of the fear in my stomach into anger. Jax didn't deserve this. Not now, not ever. He was a good guy. I couldn't let Sarah get away, leaving Jax to wonder what he'd done wrong again. I wouldn't let that happen.

"You're evil," I said.

"Yeah, yeah." She rolled her eyes. "You were always Miss Mother Theresa, weren't you? I was quite surprised when you came back as a stripper with purple hair."

"It's *ombré*," I said. "And I'm not a stripper. You should know that. You took my class."

"Enough chitchat. I'm getting bored, and I've got a flight to catch." Sarah raised the gun and glanced at me. Her finger crooked back.

"Wait." I called out. "Tell me one thing."

Sarah's finger relaxed. "What?"

"Why did you do it? Why kill Anthony and blame me?"

"You really haven't put it together?" Sarah's hand remained steady.

"Some of it..." I paused.

But obviously Sarah didn't want to indulge me, judging by her twitching trigger finger.

I took that as my cue to start talking before Sarah shut me up permanently. "Let me guess, then. You moved back here from somewhere—you mentioned you went to San Diego. Did you live there?"

Sarah's expression was somewhat less than mildly amused, but she didn't comment. A lightbulb clicked on in my head.

"You got into the whole cosplay thing in San Diego. Then when you moved back here. Maybe you missed it, or maybe you needed extra cash...or something," I said, gaining steam as Sarah's eyebrow lifted. "Then, for whatever reason, you found out about the underground comic shop in Little Lake."

"Pretty good, actually. In fact, I met Anthony in San Diego. He mentioned that if I ever moved back, he had an opportunity for me in Little Lake. Good money, easy hours, fun job," she said. "I was pretty bored of traveling around by that time, and I wanted to buy a house. So I came back."

"But you didn't have a job, so you took up Anthony's offer for some quick cash," I added. "And then it turned out to be more than you bargained for. It started as innocent costume stuff, but Anthony wanted more. Did he pay you to sleep with him?"

"I'm not a *prostitute*." Sarah's eyes flamed. "I loved him. Shut your mouth, Misty. I don't ever want to hear you say that again. I loved Anthony, and he loved me."

"But apparently he didn't love you enough to leave his wife for you." I pressed onward, mostly because Sarah seemed to have forgotten about the gun in her anger, and it drooped to point at my midsection. I could maybe survive if the gun went off at that angle.

"He was *going* to leave her." Sarah looked a bit uncomfortable. "He kept promising me."

"But you gave him an ultimatum?" I asked.

"He waited too long! It wasn't my fault. He got the inheritance, and he was going to have to split it with the old witch because he didn't leave her in time. That money was supposed to be for me and Anthony. We were going to go away to San Diego, or the Bahamas—someplace warm. Because we loved each other."

"He wasn't going to go," I said quietly. "You realized it. And he wasn't going to give you his money."

Sarah raised the gun. "That's right, asshole. People aren't who you think they are. Ask Jax. I'll bet he was surprised when you left him ten years ago. Really broke his heart, you know. He still talks about it. Cries, even. Embarrassing for a grown man."

I leapt forward. I didn't care about the gun. The feeling of hatred inside me had been bubbling up ever since I'd seen Sarah again, latent after years and years gone past, back to when she'd stolen my tooth at the tender age of five. I guess she'd just been born a bad apple.

But now, the rate at which my anger increased had gone up exponentially since we'd entered the garage, and I wanted to grab her, shake her until she was scared and breathless, until she said she was sorry for hurting Jax, and for killing the Jenkinses, and for ruining my studio.

Her eyes widened, but before I could get to her, there was a shot.

I crashed into Sarah, the gun clattering to the ground as her hand flew to the side of her head.

"Ow, goddamn it! I'm shot!" Sarah wrestled me off her, but I had years of resentment built up inside, and I pinned her to the ground. I kicked the gun out of reach, wondering who in the heck had shot at Sarah. And if it had been a bullet, why she wasn't dead.

A noise in the bushes drew my attention, and I looked up to see Donna walking toward me holding Harmony's BB gun.

"Donna!" I said. "What are you doing?"

She gave a sheepish smile. "I didn't trust you not to go in, so I drove home and called the station. I explained quickly to Jax and Nathan everything they needed to know, and then I came right back here. This was the only thing I could find," she said, raising the BB gun. "I don't allow guns in the house, and you'd brought this over with Harmony yesterday."

"I'm buying you two steaks," I said. "You're a rock star."

"Bitch, that hurt," Sarah said, still struggling to throw me off of her.

I concentrated my efforts on keeping her down. Donna gave her another shot, this time to the thigh.

"The next one is in your eyeball," Donna said. "So don't move. And I have a few questions myself."

"You do?" I asked.

"You bet I do," Donna said, looking none too happy. "Sarah, did you steal my sunflowers? I left those for Misty. But when I stopped by Jax's place and ran into Sarah, I saw some looking suspiciously like them sitting on his kitchen table."

Sarah rolled her eyes.

"Did you?" Donna pressed.

"Yes, fine. It was too easy to pin it on that creep, Alfie."

"Alfie didn't have the sunflowers in his backpack when he left that day?" I asked. "I assumed he did."

"It was probably his stupid costume in the bag," Sarah said. "He carried that thing everywhere."

"What about the break-in at my house? Did you get someone to do that?" I asked.

"No, that was all me. I took Jax's cop car. He didn't even notice, and again, Alfie was too easy," Sarah said. "The people in this town make it *so* easy to commit a crime!"

"It was you that called the station and tipped off the cops after class, and the first phone call about Mr. Jenkins's body— that was you, too, wasn't it?" I asked, things slowly falling into place. "I thought it was nosy Barbara who called after class, spilling her guts about Mrs. Jenkins's odd comments. And it was *you* I passed on the day my studio was vandalized." I shook my head. "And when you broke into my house, was it to steal another stocking?"

Sarah rolled her eyes. "Very good. A-plus as usual. Still the straight A student you were all your life, except now it doesn't matter anymore."

"Did you kill Mrs. Jenkins with the stocking?" I asked.

"I didn't kill her. At least...she's not dead yet. Unlike Anthony. All it took for that man was a tiny bit of seduction, and he was all mine..." Sarah winced as Donna prodded her with the tip of the BB gun.

I stood up and jabbed a foot into Sarah's back. "Where is she?"

"I'm not saying. She'll be dead soon anyway. And I have full confidence you'll find her in the very near future," Sarah said.

"Where is she?" I jabbed my foot again.

Sarah frowned but didn't break down. "It was a shame, really. All that effort to break into your house, and I barely got to use the stocking. In fact, Mrs. Jenkins had a lot more fight left in her than Anthony."

My stomach churned at how easily Sarah could describe killing people. Her voice didn't waver. Her eyes didn't flicker with regret—there was simply nothing. She could've been describing the chemical makeup of a rock, and her tone would've been fitting.

"You're gonna be spending your life in prison," a voice said from behind the garage. "So you might as well do it with two eyes. You have three seconds to tell us where Mrs. Jenkins is being held, or else I'm turning around while Donna carries out her promise to aim for your eyeballs," Jax said, his voice flat.

I turned and made eye contact with Jax, who must have been hiding behind the garage. He emerged from the side walkway, holding a gun out in front of him, a mask of stone covering his features.

"Jax," Sarah said. "These women—"

"Don't start. I've heard everything."

"Everything?" I asked, wincing a bit, remembering the bits about me sticking up for Jax, defending him, all the lovey-dovey stuff. I couldn't remember all of what had been said aloud, and what I'd kept to myself. The moment was already a blur of emotions, nerves, and adrenaline.

"Everything. There's time to discuss *that* later." Jax's tone was final. He held the gun close to his former lover's head. "Right now I'm waiting to hear where you've left Mrs. Jenkins."

Sarah's mouth remained shut. "Jax, you wouldn't."

"Donna, I'm turning around now. I encourage you to *not* shoot Sarah in the face, but if you miss her thigh, there's not much I can do about it." Jax nodded at me. "You're a witness, right? You'll back me up that Donna's aim is terrible, and she *accidentally* shot Sarah in the eyeball in self-defense?"

I nodded. "Donna's life was definitely in danger. It's completely self-defense."

"I've been waiting for action like this forever." Donna lifted the gun, her finger on the trigger, balancing sights and taking aim.

"Wait. Fine." Sarah squinted. "The studio. She's in your studio."

"My studio?" I asked. "Seriously, haven't you done enough to it?"

"She's done enough forever," Jax said. Speaking to the back of the garage, Jax continued. "Guys…bring her in. I'm headed over to the studio to get Mrs. Jenkins."

"I'm coming too," I said, glancing around to see how many other cops had been waiting out back.

"Me too." Donna let the BB gun fall to her side.

"No, Donna, you've seen enough. You've helped more than I could've asked for. Just go home to your kids. I'll let you know what we find," I said.

Donna looked as if she were about to refuse flat out, but she glanced down at the BB gun and paused. "Alec was coughing…I should probably see how he's doing."

"Go. Thank you for everything. Go to your kids." I gave Donna a hug. "You've saved my life enough times today—I promise. There'll be plenty more opportunities for life-saving later."

"The kids are with the neighbor now. She was more than happy to help out," Nathan added. "Don't worry, you've got a bit of time."

"It was my pleasure. Plus, I really wanted a steak. You owe me one." Donna smiled, kissed me on one cheek, and then moved over to where her husband held down Sarah.

Nathan kissed his wife on the cheek. "You know, babe, all you gotta do is ask next time you want me to barbecue. I'll make you a steak so you can avoid this whole Batman, superhero sort of thing."

"I want to get fancy and go out," Donna said. "Get some drinks. Can you make that happen?"

"Done," Nathan said.

"Get in line, buddy. I got a date with your wife first." I smiled.

Nathan sighed. "I'll never win."

"Let's go." Jax reached out and pulled me away, dragging me into his squad car.

We passed Donna jumping into her mom van and heading home and Sarah being loaded into a different squad car. We were halfway across town before Jax spoke.

"What was all that love of your life talk?" Jax asked suddenly.

"That was Sarah speaking," I said. "She's the one who said you were the love of my life."

"Was she right?"

"About which part?" I hedged.

"Do I ask for commitment too fast?" Jax refused to glance at me, staring straight through his front window.

"No." I looked over, sliding my hand onto his and giving it a light squeeze. "You don't. I made a mistake. And Sarah was a psycho. I should've known, since she had crazy eyes. Why do you go for girls with crazy eyes?"

"The ones with the crazy eyes are best in bed," he said, a small smile quirking up the sides of his lips for the first time in a while.

"Oh, thanks." I rolled my eyes. "I must have bored you, then. I definitely don't have crazy eyes."

"What do you mean?" Jax winked. "Sweetheart, you were the best I ever had." Jax gave a half smirk, his gaze still focused on the road, hands on the wheel.

I glanced at Jax, partially flattered and mostly flustered. Before I could comment, we'd reached my studio.

"This is to be continued," I said.

Jax got out of the car and headed toward the entrance. I scurried behind him, mostly afraid of what I would find inside my studio. Hopefully the last gruesome surprise for a long, long time.

"You don't have to come in." Jax turned to me, one hand on the door of the studio, one hand clasped around my wrist. His eyes were downcast.

"I'm coming with you." I waited until he raised his eyes to meet mine.

When he finally met my gaze, his eyes were wary. "I'm sorry. I should've known that Sarah was...that she wasn't..."

"It's not your fault. She fooled all of us. You can't feel bad about it," I said, reaching out and resting a hand on his shoulder.

"There were signs...but I just—I didn't want it to be true. With you back in town..." He looked over his shoulder toward the studio door. "I had to keep my mind off of you. I thought dating someone else would do the trick."

I waited, sensing he wasn't done.

"It didn't work, *and* it made me blind to the things I should have been noticing from the start. It was all a mistake."

"It's okay, Jax." I put my hand on his chest. "Let's talk more about this later. We have to see if Mrs. Jenkins is alive."

He nodded. "You've seen enough. You don't have to come in here."

"I want to," I said with a deep breath.

Jax pushed open the door to the studio, and I stepped through behind him, my breath lodged somewhere in my throat.

All was silent in the studio. There were no words scrawled across the mirror in red, no blood splattered on the floor. In fact, it looked just as clean as when I'd left it after my last class.

"Was she lying?" I whispered. "What if she's not here?"

"I don't see why she would." Jax walked around. "What does she have to gain from lying? She thought Mrs. Jenkins would already be dead by the time we got here, so it wouldn't have made a difference."

I paused. "It makes sense that Mrs. Jenkins would be here. Sarah was trying to pin her murder on me, so it's a logical choice, really."

"But where?" Jax asked.

There was one spare feather floating across the floor. I moved toward it, doubting that Sarah was telling the truth. There was no sign of a struggle anywhere. With the amount of blood in Mrs. Jenkins's house, how could Sarah have dragged a still-alive, possibly struggling Mrs. Jenkins through here with no sign of anything wrong?

Another feather drifted across the floor. It must have been coming from the costume closet. My head jerked toward it. *The costume closet!*

I hustled back, Jax calling after me as I yanked the door open. Where normally feather boas and sequins prevailed, today, amid the sparkles and men's button-up shirts, sat a bound and gagged figure.

"Mrs. Jenkins!" I said.

She mumbled a response through the feather boa stuffed in her mouth.

"Here, Jax," I said, struggling to free the woman from her bindings.

Jax was by my side by the time I removed the gag from her mouth, and within two seconds, he had removed a knife and slashed through the rope around her wrists and her hands.

"You're alive," I said. "Thank God."

"Of course I'm alive," Mrs. Jenkins growled. "How else would the little bitch get my money?"

"What?" I looked at Jax.

He shot a puzzled gaze back at me.

"I thought y'all would've figured it out by now." Mrs. Jenkins massaged her wrists as Jax helped her to her feet outside of the closet. "Y'all are slower than I thought."

"Did Sarah bring you here?" I asked.

"Very good, Sherlock." Mrs. Jenkins rolled her head in a slow circle. "Really cricked my neck being tied up in there."

"But are you hurt? What about the blood?" I scanned Mrs. Jenkins for signs of bullet holes or other injuries that released lots of blood. However, with the exception of the crick in her neck and a rather grumpy disposition, Mrs. Jenkins appeared to be unscathed.

"What blood?" she asked. "I don't know what you're talking about. I'm no use to the girl *dead*."

At our blank gazes, she continued, cackling the whole while. "Oh, come on. Sarah would *never* find the money if she killed me."

"The inheritance?" I asked.

She nodded. "Anthony and I had a less-than-perfect marriage, sure. He cheated on me, stayed out a little too late, but the old coot loved me."

I tried my best not to let my face show surprise.

Mrs. Jenkins shifted. "And I loved him, too.. Well, I hated him. It was complicated. He wasn't ever gonna leave me. And when he got that money, we thought maybe we could make things work again. Take some time off. Rekindle the ol' spark."

She leaned forward and winked. "You saw that ol' photo when you was in my place. I was a looker back in the day. I just had to make him remember that so he didn't go chasing some younger tail."

"He shouldn't have cheated on you," I said. "You're...you're not *old* tail."

Mrs. Jenkins shook her finger. "You won't ever understand. He wasn't perfect, but he loved me. I promise you that. And we was gonna use the money for our second honeymoon. But when he told that girl about it, she got jealous and killed him straight off. Tried to pin it on you—I haven't figured that one out, except for maybe you was convenient—"

"She's hated me since we were five," I added.

Jax gave me a look.

I shrugged. "It's true! She stole my tooth."

Mrs. Jenkins nodded. "She was just a bad apple."

"I wonder what all that blood was about," I said. "It looked like a massacre happened in your place."

"Probably wasn't even blood," she said. "Anthony had a bottle of that fake junk in his closet. The stuff for Halloween costumes. He needed it for something, not sure what."

I looked at Jax. "Wouldn't the crime scene guys have figured that out already?"

"They may have. I haven't talked with them since I left to arrest you."

"The costumes," I said, realization kicking in. "Wow. We thought you were dead."

"Well, I ain't. I'm alive and kicking, and I'm gonna go on home now," she said. "Use some of that money for a massage."

"Uh, Mrs. Jenkins, we're going to have to take you in for a statement," Jax said.

"How about this as a statement?" She held up her hand with one finger—the middle one—pointing straight to the heavens. "Pass that along to the girl, why don't ya?"

"*Hm*," Jax said, hiding a smile. "Well, I can't exactly write that on the record, so I'm sorry, but you'll have to come down to the station with us. I'll tell you what—we'll take you down there, treat you real nice, and get you a cup of coffee, and in the meantime send a crew over to clean up your place. It's a real mess in there."

"If you add some Bailey's and vodka to the coffee, you've got a deal," Mrs. Jenkins huffed. "And I don't need a cleaning crew. I'm getting myself a new place, right in the city center. I got plenty of money now."

"That's great!" I said.

As Mrs. Jenkins and Jax swiveled their heads to look at me, I realized how my excitement could *potentially* come off the wrong way. "I mean...I'm glad you'll be able to afford a new place, but it's terrible the price at which it came."

Jax gave a slight shake of his head in disbelief. Mrs. Jenkins continued to stare, until Jax prodded her, saying, "You've got a deal with the coffee and vodka. Let's get this over with."

The two began to walk toward the door, leaving me to shut the costume closet and glance around at my studio once more. It wasn't the horrific scene I'd pictured, thankfully. Mrs. Jenkins was alive. Jax was safe, despite his psychotic girlfriend, and my studio remained intact. Only Sarah hadn't fared so well. But I wasn't all too sad about that.

"Do you need a ride home?" Jax asked from the doorway.

"No, I'm going to stay here for a bit. Clean up, get some stuff done." I shrugged. "Go ahead. I'll find my way home later."

"I'll see you in class on Monday," Mrs. Jenkins said. "These hips aren't getting any younger. I gotta keep 'em nice and loose."

She did a little sashay with her hips, and Jax's eyes widened to the size of golf balls before he hightailed it out of the room, not appearing to care whether or not Mrs. Jenkins followed him anymore.

"See you," I said, with a small wave. I couldn't help the grin playing across my lips. Maybe there was time for things to turn around in Little Lake. Maybe all hope wasn't lost yet.

CHAPTER EIGHTEEN

———

"All right, now toss your shirt forward. Be a tease. If you're dancing for someone else, get your partner involved." I demonstrated by flicking my wrist and letting the oversized men's shirt fly from my fingers into the front row of my students.

A classroom full of students followed suit, and I smiled amid sixteen shirts flying toward the mirror at the front of the studio.

After Mrs. Jenkins had given her statement, Sarah had been booked at the jailhouse, and I had been relieved of all charges against me (they let the whole *breaking out of jail* thing slip since I'd been an integral part in capturing Sarah). Life in Little Lake had improved.

In fact, Mrs. Jenkins had showed up with a pile of cash in hand (she didn't believe in banks or checks, apparently) as a donation to the burlesque fund of Little Lake. I told her no such thing existed, but she insisted on donating the money anyway.

"This town could use a little sexiness," she said. "Plus, without you I'd still be locked up in that closet spitting up feathers. Take it."

I nearly toppled beneath the weight of the sack containing the money. "I can't possibly take this. Buy yourself a new house. Go on a trip. You deserve it."

"I'm doing both. This is only a tenth of the money I got in the inheritance."

My mind was boggled. "Was Anthony descended from royalty?"

"Something like that. I didn't really pay attention." Mrs. Jenkins shrugged. "I didn't marry him for his money. He had a huge..."

"Okay, okay, thank you." I accepted the money and grimaced.

"...had a huge heart," she finished, a sly grin on her face.

"Are you sure you don't want to use the money for anything else?" I asked, feeling uncomfortable accepting it.

"Consider it a donation in my honor. All I want is a lifetime of free classes," she said.

"Wow. Of course. I'm...I'm speechless. Thank you," I said, my voice cracking.

"You've got guts, girl. You deserve it. I'm sure you'll use it wisely." Mrs. Jenkins nodded.

I was incredibly touched by Mrs. Jenkins's gesture, and I told her so.

"Stop being sentimental, or I'm taking it all back. Stick with sexy," she said.

"Got it." I smiled. "See you in class on Monday?"

"Course," she growled, leaving the studio without a backward glance. "And don't tell anyone where you got the money from."

With the money, I'd been able to clean up the studio, pay off some debts, and even get a working business phone line. My personal line, I was happy to announce, had been ringing off the hook about classes. I'd been able to put up some advertisements around town, and the classes had even been announced in the church bulletin, to my surprise.

Donna brought the bulletin to me after Mass on Sunday, shoving it in my hands and whispering in my ear. "Tell me you did *not* threaten Father Olaf again to get this advertisement."

"No! What are you talking about?" I glanced down at the bulletin. "I didn't threaten him, but that's *awesome*."

Donna leaned over and whispered, "Maybe he felt bad. I heard he and Alfie got a little *talking to* at the station over the weekend. Alfie got a slap on the wrist and a bit of desk duty."

Somehow, over the weekend word had spread, the chatter around town enticing students to check out my studio. And now, in my Monday class, I had all sorts of folks dancing to all sorts of songs. The signups had increased exponentially, and I'd even had to open two more classes. One intermediate and a second beginner, in order to accommodate the demand.

"Great class today," I said, scanning the crowd. Nosy Barbara Jones was back, along with the rest of my initial beginner's class, minus Sarah. Mrs. Jenkins was rocking a cutoff-jean miniskirt with a flimsy little sports bra.

"I'll see you all next week! Practice on a partner or practice alone. Whatever you do, have fun with it!"

My class filed out of the room, the light chatter music to my ears, the shiny faces of happy students warming my heart.

As soon as the last student was gone, I set to sweeping up the layer of feathers coating the floor. I hummed a little ditty, shaking my booty a bit as I did so. Life was good right now. Life was more than good.

"Nice moves," a voice rumbled from the doorway.

I spun around to see Jax leaning against the doorframe. But this time, I smiled at the sight of him. "Thinking of joining my class?"

"I'm not cut out to be a stripper. Though I do have handcuffs, if you're interested in testing them out."

"I'm not a *stripper*." I crossed my arms. "Get it right. Father Olaf wouldn't be advertising a stripping class in his bulletin."

"I wouldn't be so sure. He's scared senseless of you. I'm pretty sure he'd advertise anything you asked him to."

"I didn't *ask* him to advertise anything."

"Except stripping."

"It's. Not. Stripping." I put my hands on my hips.

"Then you better show me a routine so I can be the judge of that."

"Ha," I retorted, going back to sweeping.

"Or, you can go out with me on Friday."

I opened my mouth then shut it again.

"What do you say—how about a date?" He took a few steps forward into the room.

"I can't go out with you on Friday," I said.

Jax scratched his chin and looked up at the ceiling. "Are you being difficult on purpose, or do you not want to go out with me?"

I paused. "I already have a date on Friday."

"Oh. Well, in that case..." Jax gave a smile, but it didn't light up his face. It hurt my heart a bit. "Let me know if that doesn't work out."

"I'm taking Harmony shooting," I said, with a smile. "I promised her a date. Then I promised Donna I'd buy her two steaks and double that number of martinis. So, I'm booked on Friday. But Saturday I'm free."

Jax smiled. "Saturday it is. Unless, of course, you need some supervision with the guns on Friday?"

"It's just a BB gun," I said.

"It's just a date," Jax said, taking a few steps toward me.

I didn't have a follow up as we stood a foot apart, eyeing each other warily. We'd both been hurt before. By one another, as well as others. It'd been ten years since we'd been in the same space, both unattached—neither arresting the other for murder. It was a strange, new feeling. A bit uncomfortable, but one I could learn to enjoy again.

He put his arm around me, and the awkward silence vanished. We hugged tightly, our bodies fitting together just so, his lips brushing against my neck and sending tingles to all ends of my nerves. My heart beat a bit faster, and my stomach fluttered from the close contact. And when his lips met mine, the world around me went dark.

Some eternity later, Jax pulled away from me. "I'm glad it wasn't you after all."

I rolled my eyes. "Did you ever think it was?"

Jax shrugged. "Not really. But mostly because I didn't think orange was your color."

"Good. I'll wear blue to our date."

"How about one of these?" Jax bent over and scooped up an extra-large men's button-up shirt. "The rest is optional."

ABOUT THE AUTHOR

Originally from St. Paul, Minnesota, Gina LaManna has also called Italy and Los Angeles home. At the moment she lives nine blocks from the beach and sometimes runs marathons. After studying numbers and equations in college, she realized multiple choice tests were "just not for her" and began writing books instead. She loves cappuccino foam and whipped cream and would subsist solely on sprinkles if possible. She has one imaginary dog.

Gina also writes the *Mini Pie the Spy!* books, under the pen name, Libby LaManna, a children's series featuring an over-enthusiastic little detective, similar in style to Junie B. Jones.

To learn more about Gina, visit her online at www.ginalamanna.com

Enjoyed this book? Check out these books available in print now from Gemma Halliday Publishing:

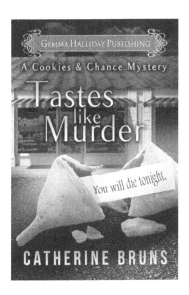

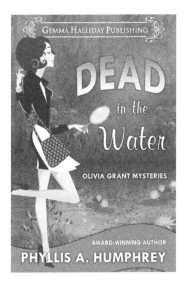

Made in the USA
Coppell, TX
12 April 2022

76445787R00111